THE

mommy
clique

Peggy,
Thanks for your support.
Happy reading!
Barbra Altamirano

THE
mommy
clique

BARBARA ALTAMIRANO

atmosphere press

CHAPTER ONE

ELISE

I decided to give it a try, just for kicks. After all, how hard could it be? All I had to do was keep walking. *Don't look back. Don't turn. Just keep going,* I told myself.

Walking down the hallway, I stared straight ahead. I could do this. I took one step. Then another. I resisted the temptation to gaze at the glamour shot from my wedding. I resisted turning into the living room, where my collector Barbie dolls awaited my attention, encased safely away in their place of honor. These were encouraging signs, but I had another even more difficult goal. Now, even with the stairs, all I had to do was look to the right and call to Brianna. I was home free.

Suddenly, I knew I couldn't do it. I spun the other way and gazed into the entryway mirror. I wasn't disappointed. The woman before me was pure perfection. What was the use of false modesty? There was no denying the truth.

Earlier Jordan had seen me at the mirror, and I caught her rolling her eyes in the reflection. I'd turned and stared her down. I understood only too well that parenting was not a delicate balance. It was simply about power—maintaining my power so they always knew who was boss.

Jordan, with that eye roll, had actually meant, "Really? You're always either looking at yourself in the mirror or staring at your Barbies." I knew because she'd said as much before. I did not bother to explain, again, that my dolls were actually collectors' items and worth thousands.

And neither did I get into any kind of discussion trying to justify looking at myself in the mirror. What was wrong with that anyway? Nothing.

With some satisfaction, I saw that at least Jordan would not speak her thoughts out loud. She did, however, return my gaze with little sign of acquiescence—or fear.

My two girls were so different. Jordan took after Brad looks-wise, while Brianna was my true replica. I didn't play favorites; I simply couldn't help but notice how Brad's features, so attractive on him, were too masculine for Jordan's face. Brianna, on the other hand, was feminine and dainty, already a lovely girl who would grow into a stunning young woman.

Jordan might be her mother's daughter in one way, however—toughness. And after all, that wasn't a bad thing; it could serve her well in life as it had for me.

When Jordan had turned away from me, I'd noticed her hips. Although still slender, thank God, I detected a little more ... curviness. It was too soon to be worried, but heaven knew I could not have a heavy daughter on my hands. I would have no idea how to deal with that particular problem, no well of personal experience to draw from.

I did know, just from watching the experience of the less fortunate, that there were at least three kisses of death when it came to popularity in school—acne, weight issues, and insecurity or shyness. Really it was, as in nature, all about survival of the fittest. Those with the best attributes rose to the top, which was only right and natural.

I was doing my best to help my daughters avoid these all-too-real pitfalls, but then they did have my, and Brad's, genes on their side. My guess was they'd be just fine.

Regardless, I decided I'd make something out of my South Beach Diet cookbook tonight, for Jordan and me. Brianna I didn't have to worry about because she never had much of an appetite—a lucky trait for a girl. As for Brad, he'd want something else, so I'd probably have to serve two dinners. It was slightly annoying but then it was good to keep him satisfied. No one in the neighborhood, or perhaps even the whole town, had a husband to rival him looks-wise. He was the perfect accompaniment for me: he always looked so good on my arm. I was, rightfully, very proud of that fact.

As if he'd heard his name in my thoughts, I heard Brad's steps on the staircase. He passed by me and grabbed my butt. He started to pull his hand away, but then stopped like it was Velcroed to my perfect posterior. The guy could never leave me alone. That was surely proof that I had nothing to worry about where he was concerned, that he had no reason to have wandering eyes.

He slid his arms around me, but I shrugged him off. "Brad, please. You'll mess up my outfit."

Brad put his hands on my waist and rubbed up against me.

I pushed him away again. "Stop acting like a horny teenager." Normally I wouldn't mind but I worried that he'd damaged my carefully crafted look. Checking the mirror again I saw there was no significant damage from his ... attentions.

I pulled out the lipstick I kept in the entryway cabinet and added another coat of my favorite shade—ruby red. "I need to be perfect today. Since I hear there will be some fresh meat." There was a new mom in the neighborhood. And being the head of the ... welcoming committee ... one could say, I was looking forward to showing her just what this 'hood was made of. Beautiful, strong women, like me.

In the mirror I saw Brad's eyebrows come together. "Fresh meat? You're going to the meat store? How about steak tonight?" He narrowed his eyes playfully. "Wait. You messing around with the butcher?"

"The butcher? Please. He's not in my league."

"How about the mailman?"

"Ditto." I smiled and left the mirror, grabbing my designer handbag. "But if you ask me about the UPS guy, I've got no comment."

"So, dinner?" Brad took my former station by the mirror. He stared at himself, fixing his shirt and inspecting his face with preoccupied fascination.

I sighed. "I'll get steak." He didn't even notice my UPS remark.

In fact, he was still busy at the mirror, totally engrossed in what he saw there. I put my arms around his waist now, drawing his attention back where it belonged.

He turned and gave me what passed for a quick kiss for him, his tongue jamming down my throat, then went immediately back to the mirror. I managed to avoid rolling my eyes.

"Filet mignon, okay, Elise? Not some cheap stuff."

I sighed again. Food was definitely a way to keep this man happy. True, there were a couple other ways, but food was the most direct line. The man could eat like a pig and still look good while I had to watch whatever I put in my mouth. Keeping this perfect figure took work. Still, it was worth it.

"Brianna, hurry up," I called up the stairs in a reasonable voice. I refused to yell. Yelling was for parents who were not in control. "We'll be late."

She appeared at the top of the stairs, looking fashionable, cute, and annoyed. "We don't have to leave yet, Mommy, do we?"

"Yes, we do. We're always on time. You know the rule."

She rolled her eyes as she ambled down. "I know, I know. On time and lookin' fine."

Her eye roll unnerved me a bit. She was in first grade. Wasn't that early for eye rolls? Was Jordan's middle school combativeness rubbing off on Brianna? I hoped not.

Brad laughed and held out his hand for a fist bump with Brianna. "You got it. Two of my finest girls." He smiled and winked at me.

What did that mean? Who else was his girl? He wouldn't be so careless to say that, if there actually were ... another girl. As in a girlfriend or a ... mistress? But of course, there wasn't ...

Brad watched me as his lips turned up in amusement. "Jordan's my girl, too, you know."

Oh—Jordan. Of course that's what he meant.

Really, it was silly of me to doubt him. I trusted him. Completely. Anyway, Brad would have to be crazy to cheat with all of this—I faced the mirror again—available to him every night. No, I was safe. The danger years were approaching, but there was always Botox. And if—heaven forbid—I started sagging, there was silicone. But I didn't think it would come to that. I had good genes. Everywhere.

Brianna got her backpack, and soon we were on our way. I strode to the car, feeling almost giddy. It had been a long, boring summer. But now, finally, it was showtime.

RONNIE

"Nick, we have to get out there. Now," I ordered. "Jessie, move it. I don't want to be late."

I stood holding the door open and finally they ran out, one after the other. Jessie tripped on the way out because, as always, she had a book in her hand. The girl was smart, no doubt about it. I smiled. Just like her mom. But maybe, unlike her mom, she'd use her intellect for good.

I harbored an uncanny feeling that Jessica—I allowed the nickname Jessie now, but when older she would use her full name—would accomplish great things. Although I suspected this hoping for greatness was fairly typical, I knew not many actually achieve it. But I believed Jessie had it in her. I was also self-aware enough to know I wanted this greatness not only for her but for me as well.

Greatness aside, I did sincerely hope she would avoid using her intelligence for petty reasons, engaging in secret machinations and other devious behavior. Or worse yet, pretending not to be smart. I remembered girls who sunk to that sad trick in order to get boys in high school, but that was something I could not abide in my daughter. As to the question of how I'd used my own intellect, I refused to dwell on it. A person did what they had to.

I shook my head, trying to pull myself out of these strange thoughts. It wasn't like I was an evil sorceress or something. Maybe I'd been reading Jessie too many princess stories lately. I made a mental note to load up on nonfiction later at the library.

Luckily, we didn't have far to go, since the bus stop was on our corner. Despite what I told the kids, we were never late; in fact, we were almost always first. I knew

Elise preferred that distinction, but even though I knew it was petty, I liked to beat her in this one way at least. Maybe it was because there were so many ways that I had to let it appear that she had beaten me. I knew my being first bothered her, perfectionist that she is, although she would never admit to it.

Sure enough, from my perch on the lawn, I watched Elise get out of her car with a small frown on her face. However, when she caught my eye, it quickly changed to a smile that appeared almost genuine.

Kelly, Elise's sidekick and ever-present companion, pulled into her usual spot—right behind her. It was an all-too-appropriate spot. Kelly always had Elise's back, yet she was never first in any way, never daring to outshine her majesty. They chatted with each other briefly and headed over. It was the usual drill. Elise never walked alone.

Their two daughters looked great, as always. They were two perfect-looking girls who belonged on the cover of *American Girl* or, although only seven, some beauty magazine for the under-thirteen crowd. Sometimes I couldn't help but think it wasn't fair. Although my daughter was cute, she just wasn't in their league looks-wise. Thanks to me, my daughter was in their clique—I had worked hard to get her there. Yet sometimes I wondered how safe she was. Brianna and Diana—their names even rhymed—were future cheerleaders. My daughter was a future debate club member. I was smart enough to know that wasn't a bad thing. It bothered me anyway.

"Ronnie, how are you?" Elise asked. Before I could answer she went on, "How was your summer?"

"It was great, we went to the Cape ..."

"Oh, how ... sweet. The Cape is just so ... charming.

Really, it's just perfect for you. Kelly and I went on a European cruise. Girls, why don't you tell Jessie all about it? I'm sure she would love to hear all about our trip."

There it was. The first dig of the year. I had to hand it to Elise—she was good. You were never really sure whether she was insulting you or being nice. She was so smooth and always had a friendly smile on her face. Well, almost always. Only a history with her told you the real story.

I wanted to turn the conversation. "Did you hear about the new family?" I'd heard too, but it was always good to find out what Elise knew.

Elise smiled like a Cheshire cat. "Yes. The father has dark skin. Maybe Hispanic or Middle Eastern. The mom is white." She paused as if waiting for us to respond, possibly with shock.

But what did she think this was, the '60s? Yes, up till now, this was a totally white neighborhood, but did she have to act like she was a card-carrying member of the KKK? Not that it wasn't possible.

Kelly jumped into the brief silence. "Really, he has dark skin? But she's Caucasian?" Her voice held sufficient shock, and Elise nodded to her, a satisfied gleam in her eye.

I fought to keep from rolling my eyes. I knew more, as I always did, and I offered a tidbit. "The last name is Tapia. So, I'm guessing Hispanic." Duh, people. Was I the only one here who did their homework?

"There's a little girl, same age. And a baby, I think," Kelly added.

I knew about the children. There was an older son, a teenager. But I kept that to myself.

Elise smiled again. "It should be fun."

I smiled back, but it was an effort. Didn't the woman ever get tired of the same old shenanigans? Didn't she ever want to start acting like a grown woman instead of the lead actress in some bad teenage movie? The whole thing was so high school. It was odd to think that now as a thirty-something woman, I'd gotten myself involved in this cliquey group with all the teenage intrigue. I'd managed to avoid this stuff in high school—for the most part. If anything, my group of the best and brightest had been the targets, not the predators. I refused to think about that any deeper. That part of my life was long over.

Yet now here I was smack dab in the middle of all this teenage-y popularity junk. How had that managed to happen?

It didn't matter how I'd gotten here because I knew I had to keep playing my part. What else could I do? And, after all, I was good at it. I'd continue to let Elise think she was the best, but in actuality that "honor" went to me. It was all part of the game to keep that fact to myself.

GAIL

"Shit," I mumbled.

"What did you say, Mommy?" Nina asked from the backseat of the car.

"Er. Shoot, sweetie. I said shoot."

"It didn't sound like that. It sounded like ..."

I struggled not to shout out of annoyance. "I said shoot and that's it." I looked over at the group already assembled on the corner and mumbled, "Why do they have to get here so freaking early?"

"Freaking? Daddy says that's a bad word."

"He's right." Thanks, Joe. "Forget it ... come on, sweetie. We have to hurry."

"Why? The bus isn't even here yet."

"No. And it won't be for a while. But everyone else is for some stupid reason."

"Stupid? Daddy says ..."

"Oh, shush! Come on, let's go."

I got Nina out and we made our way over. I strode toward them but made it look casual. I wouldn't rush. I knew not to do that, at least. Last year had taught me a thing or two. Or three or ... well, a lot anyway.

They didn't look at me as I approached. But they'd seen me. It was the same old routine. As I came up next to Ronnie, she smiled in my direction, slightly. Elise finished her sentence and then turned to me.

"Gail, how are you?" She waited a beat, then went on, "Same old Gail, I see." She laughed like we were sharing some private joke. "Having a hard time getting Nina away from ... what's that show you let her watch?"

Shit. First day of the year and she already thinks I'm going to be late every day. And she has to bring up the TV issue. Right. Like my kids are the only ones who had stopped watching public television.

I forced a smile. "Well, you know how it is, right?" Oh, how stupid. She didn't know how it was. She was never late. I picked at my fingernail. "Um. I meant that ..." Oh, crap. She already had me stumbling over my words.

And she knew it. Elise stared at my fidgeting hands and smiled. She patted me on the arm. "Don't worry. You have all year to work on it."

Glancing around, looking for something that I could use for a subject change, I spotted a UPS guy, one I'd seen before in the neighborhood, walking to Ronnie's house to make a delivery. This particular UPS guy was very good looking, and I thought I remembered at least one of the women in the group had talked about him before. He was kind of hard to ignore.

"Ronnie," I said, "I see you're getting a special delivery," sure that through my voice and facial expression she would get my joke.

But she just looked at me with her typical blank face. "Only some educational books I ordered for Jessie and Nick."

"But I meant the UPS guy, you know? You noticed him, right? I mean he could give Brad Pitt a run for his money." I laughed, glancing around at the others but no one else seemed to get me. Honestly, did they even have any working female hormones? Sure, we were all married women, but we weren't dead.

Then, I remembered it wasn't this group who'd talked about the UPS guy. It was my mom, blabbing with one of her friends on the phone, like always. She was such a gossip that I'd learned to limit what I told her. I knew no secret was safe with her.

I tried a different subject. "So, where's Brad?" He was always a welcome sight, too, for similar reasons.

"He was tired today," Elise answered, grinning lazily. "I let the poor guy sleep. After last night, he really needed it, if you catch my drift."

We caught it, all right. It got quiet while I'm sure every one of us imagined what it would be like to have a guy like him in our bed every night. The weird thing was I don't think Elise minded. She liked to make us all a little jealous—why else would she make comments like that? As long as we kept our fantasies just that, I'm sure she was okay with it. But either way, I doubted I could keep my mind from going there.

"But Gail, since you brought up Brad Pitt ..." Elise stopped, with a thoughtful look, then went on, "In truth, I think my Brad holds up very well in any comparison to his, well, namesake."

Kelly rushed in, "Oh, one hundred percent. Clearly, Brad Pitt has nothing on your Brad."

Crap. Was I now in trouble for making it out that Brad Pitt, or even the UPS guy, was hotter than her husband? I rushed to undue any damage. "Oh, yes, definitely. Kelly is so right about that."

Elise nodded, appearing satisfied at our words. I hoped we were good now.

Ronnie smirked, staring at something in the distance. "Don't look now, but guess who's coming to dinner?" Even though she'd just told us not to, we all looked. Well, not Elise. She was too cool for that.

Hurrying down the street was a motley crew. The mom made me feel organized, which is saying something. She was committing the cardinal sin of sprinting to the bus stop, towing her daughter along behind her. And she held a baby in her arms who kept throwing her hat. The mom would then have to stop and grab the hat and take off running again.

Elise peeked out of the corner of her eye. "This is almost too good to be true." A laugh escaped her lips.

"I mean, hello? Who walks to the bus?" That was Kelly.

"Yeah, and where's her stroller?" I put in. I was

rewarded with a smile from Elise.

"Maybe she walks to keep in shape." That was Ronnie, her face straight.

"Right. Since it's working so well for her," Elise said as we all cackled. Then she immediately shushed us. "Ladies, please. Chill." She bared her teeth, giving her next words a far different meaning. "We want our guests to feel welcome."

We knew what she meant. We needed to cool it. Soon they would be here. Elise was too smooth to be caught being catty or mean. She had her own unique style. I knew only too well just what her "style" was. I was just glad it would be directed at someone else for a change.

BETH

I took a deep breath and opened the front door. My stomach felt funky—a product of nerves no doubt. New situations were always scary, and new people even more so, but it wasn't only that. There was something about being back in the neighborhood I grew up in. Even though I knew moving back was the right thing to do, I feared encountering the ghosts of my youth. They were much better off staying dead.

I'd gone to college in Texas, seeking to become someone else, and looking for somewhere I would finally fit in. At least no one knew me there. It seemed the fresh start I craved. Only a funny thing happened: I realized no matter where I went, I was still me. I just couldn't seem to shake off the person I'd always been.

I'd met Rick senior year in college. We settled down

and had kids. But now, because of my mother's health, we'd moved back to Connecticut. I wanted my kids to spend time with her—while they could.

I stepped onto the sidewalk, staring at the ground, placing my feet tentatively. *Don't step on a crack.* Catching myself thinking this old childish saying, I made an effort to stand up taller. I remembered some boy from high school making fun of me, asking, "Why are you always staring at the ground? Looking for spare change?" I needed to fight against these old insecure habits from my youth. Now that I was living back in my hometown, I felt they might creep back into my personality, without my permission or awareness. In fact, it seemed it was already happening. I had to remind myself that I was not that scared little girl anymore.

Despite my inner pep talk, I couldn't quite force myself to ignore where I stepped. It was a silly childhood rhyme, yes, but I needed all the luck I could get on this first day of school. With my best friend from my hometown, Sara, having moved away, there was really no one I could hang out with here. I'd had a part-time job in Texas, and I was already missing the one work friend I'd made. I knew it would be nice to make a new friend here, but with getting settled and needing to help my mom and my kids, I would not be getting a job, at least not for a while. I figured the bus stop was the logical place to find another mom friend, since I'd be there everyday.

But so far the few other moms I had seen around the neighborhood hadn't seemed friendly. No one waved or smiled. Everyone drove well-kept, expensive cars. The front lawns were all immaculate, the grass so green and pure, as if the weeds and grubs wouldn't dare mess with the perfection. I'd always found perfection intimidating, whether of lawns or otherwise.

I took another step and thought of the rhyme again. Mom needed luck much more than I did. Her back was fine. Her lungs were another story. She'd been diagnosed with pulmonary fibrosis, a lung disease with no real cure. We'd spent a week on Martha's Vineyard in late June with my parents. Although it had only been a little over two months since then, she seemed weaker. But she was so happy we lived here now. When she held Kayla in her lap the other day, she'd called the baby "her cure." Despite the painful reality of her disease, I prayed it could somehow be true.

Now I couldn't afford to dwell on Mom's health. I needed to focus on soothing first-day jitters—my kids and my own. I deliberately took another step. Focusing on avoiding those cracks might have been an odd meditation but it did help divert my thoughts.

Looking up as I reached the end of the sidewalk, I swore out loud. My car wasn't in its usual spot. Vaguely I remembered Rick telling me, while still half asleep, that he was taking the car today, since he was bringing it for repairs. Borrowing his car wasn't an option because it was stick shift.

I turned and sprinted into the house, knowing I'd have to get Selena up, fed, and ready sooner than planned. Luckily the bus stop was close, so we could walk. I just did not need this hassle on the first day.

I almost ran into Ricky in the hallway as he headed out for his bus stop. "Good luck on your first day, honey."

Ricky rolled his eyes but forced out a "Thanks, Mom" before leaving the house. I forgot, now that he was a teen, he hated terms of endearment. And, it went without saying that he did not want his mother accompanying him to the bus stop. I knew he had to be nervous though. Starting a brand-new high school in a whole other part of the country would not be easy for him. Truthfully, I doubted I could've handled it. Going to the same school system my whole life had been socially challenging enough.

I knew Selena was worried. Ever since the move, she'd been clingier than usual, wanting lots of hugs from Rick and me. Ricky, on the other hand, acted like the move was no big deal. He had expressed some regret at the friends he'd be missing, but overall he acted like it was nothing he couldn't handle, reminding me of his dad's optimism and can-do attitude. Although Ricky did have much of his father in him, I suspected that his show of confidence was at least partially an act. After all, he was human.

I got Selena and the baby ready as quickly as I could and soon enough we were on our way. Holding the baby, I led Selena by the arm, trying not to pull her too hard. It seemed we must be late. A group of moms and their kids were already at the bus stop. But I had left earlier than I needed to, on purpose. *Maybe the bus company gave me the wrong time!*

"Mommy, why are you running?"

"Selena, look they're already there. Come on, hurry." I paused to pick up the baby's hat for what felt like the hundredth time. "Why does she keep taking this off?"

"Just leave it off, Mommy. Where's Kayla's stroller?"

"I don't want her face to burn. Daddy left it in the car." I was not only carless but also stroller-less. Thanks, Rick. It wasn't a long walk, but my arms were already aching.

Why did he have to take the car in for repairs on the first day of school?

"Look, there are some girls my age."

"Yes, honey. Maybe you'll make some friends." *Maybe I will too*, I thought again.

As I got closer, I noticed they looked like a tight-knit group. They were arranged in a small circle while their kids ran around unsupervised. It wasn't a busy street; still, it seemed somewhat neglectful.

I covered the distance quickly, just having to pick up the hat two more times, and soon I was two steps away from their circle. Yet no one in the group turned toward me. They were deep in conversation. This was awkward. I assumed they would notice my approach and introduce themselves. But now I could see that wasn't happening.

With no encouragement from them, I wasn't sure what to do. The other little girls had stopped playing to check out my daughter. But they weren't any friendlier. After staring at Selena for a few seconds with unsmiling faces, they went back to their playing.

I suddenly flashed back to the high school cafeteria, that year Sara wasn't in my lunch period. I'd been standing with my tray, about to flee to the bathroom, when at the last second I saw a girl I knew sitting alone. We found each other and survived.

But now seemed worse. As if sensing my unease, the baby started crying. I began rocking her, but she didn't quiet down. With all her noise, I thought for sure someone would look over. But no one did. What the hell? Was I invisible? Well, it wasn't the first time. I had that knack of blending in so well I disappeared.

The bus pulled up and the kids got in line. Selena was

last. Still not one mom had looked at me, let alone spoken to me. The baby's cries had become a full-blown wail, yet these women acted oblivious to us both.

I watched Selena get on the bus and take a seat, by herself. I waved to her and turned on my heels without a backward glance. I could play this game too. I thought of the speech I'd prepared to explain why I carried the baby— how I planned to make a joke about it. I'd forgotten the words now. It didn't matter, I wouldn't need it. Not today.

ELISE

"So, you think we got to her this morning?" Gail asked.

We were back at headquarters, waiting for the afternoon bus. The perfect-looking day with deep blue sky and a few white fluffy clouds was clearly meant for happy things. For some, that would mean a walk in the park. For others, perhaps flying kites with your kids. But I was no ordinary mom. For me it meant initiating a newbie mom.

"She went home and bawled her eyes out, no doubt," Kelly snickered.

I frowned at Kelly. "If she did, she's hardly a worthy opponent." After all, it wasn't fun if it was too easy. I think I enjoyed the challenge the most. "No, I think she's tougher than that."

"I hope so," Ronnie muttered as Gail asked at the same time, "How can you tell?"

I gave Ronnie a stare. "What's does that mean?"

"Nothing. I just hope she's not a wimp." She paused. "It just wouldn't be as much ... fun."

I had a feeling there was another reason but decided

to let it pass.

I turned to Gail. "I can tell because I saw her face when she left. She was angry, not sad. Besides, this is only the beginning. I shouldn't have to remind you. We start by ignoring. Then move into phase two."

Gail winced and looked down at her hands, picking at one of her nails. Maybe she was remembering her own "initiation." If so, good. It wouldn't hurt for her to remember her place.

Gail looked up then and smiled, putting her arms down by her side with what looked like subtle determination. "Brad still MIA?"

She'd asked about him that morning, too, I remembered. I didn't mind if the girls enjoyed his presence, to a certain degree. With the best-looking husband of the group, it was only natural that I enjoyed showing him off a bit. But it was a constant necessity to judge whether any of them was a little too interested in his comings and goings.

I forced a smile. "Yes, he's still exhausted, poor thing. But then, it's no wonder. I work him pretty hard. You know, in case his eyes should ever wander, at least he'll be too tired to do anything about it."

Kelly and Gail both rushed to speak at the same time, but Kelly spoke loudest. "Brad have wandering eyes? That would never happen, girlfriend."

I smiled, for real now. "I know. But just in case." Really, I did trust Brad. But I gave Gail a brief hard look to make sure she understood me.

"When do we move to phase two?" Kelly asked.

I glanced at Ronnie. "We'll know the right time, won't we?"

"Yes," she answered, but her eyes were not on me. They were on her daughter. Her poker face always gave little away, but now I thought she looked bored. And boredom I would not tolerate.

"We understand each other, don't we?"

"Perfectly."

I wasn't sure I liked her tone. It bordered on rebellious. But I knew she understood. And I knew I could count on her. She'd play the game—to perfection. With her uncanny ability to give away so little of what she was thinking, she was a master at it. She really would have made a great poker player. But our game was so much more interesting. Who cared about poker? I liked a game with higher stakes.

So yes, Ronnie was good. Not as good as me though. I was still—for lack of a better word—the queen. And long would I rule.

GAIL

I stood with the girls at the afternoon bus stop. Ronnie and Elise were talking to each other about the new mom and which phase we were in. Or something. But I couldn't focus on their conversation. I mean, Elise had actually glared at me when all I did was ask about Brad. I wasn't stupid; even though he was good to look at, I knew I couldn't drool over him too much, especially around Elise. But just asking about him shouldn't be off limits.

A guy from the neighborhood walked by just then, walking his dog. I'd seen him a couple times before without paying much attention. He was in his fifties I would guess, and not of a type that would really stand out.

Now, I followed him with my eyes, taking note of his broad-ish shoulders and the confident way he strode down the street. He's kind of cute, I thought.

I noticed Kelly looking at me strangely. She glanced at the man who'd just passed then back at me.

"I was just admiring his ... dog."

"Oh." Kelly looked after him. "I didn't notice. What kind of dog?"

Oh, crap. I didn't even look at the stupid dog. "Um, I don't know, probably just a mutt."

"Why would you admire a mutt?"

I shrugged. "Because it was cute? Mutts can be cute, right?"

Ronnie, apparently overhearing the last part of our conversation, suddenly spoke. "Maybe Kelly is a canine snob."

"I'm not a canine snob. And that's not a thing by the way."

Elise looked toward the man and dog now in the distance. "Gail, that dog was clearly a King Charles. Maybe you need to have your vision tested."

I was surprised Elise even saw the dog. I'd thought she was too busy talking to Ronnie to notice. But it figured. She always seemed to be one step ahead of the rest of us.

"However, I will say this: the dog was cute. The owner was another story."

The other woman all giggled. Well, he seemed kind of cute to me. Maybe I should get my vision checked.

I noticed the new mom in the distance walking toward us. After this morning I wondered what she'd do this afternoon. I wondered what she thought of us. Well. In the next few weeks she'd learn lots. Good and bad. She could decide for herself which side we belonged on. I was still working that out myself.

Elise looked at me, somewhat oddly resuming the dog conversation. "It's funny, Gail, that you think mutts are cute. Personally, I greatly prefer purebreds."

Out of the corner of my eye, I watched the new mom approaching, holding her infant. She must have thought having a babe in arms was a good conversation starter. After all, what women could resist a cute baby? These women, that's who. But she didn't know that yet.

Kelly nodded to Elise. "Oh, definitely. I agree one hundred percent."

Ronnie looked at Elise quizzically. "But you don't have a dog, do you Elise?" The new lady's steps slowed and then stopped. She stood awkwardly apart from the group. I wondered whether she'd say something.

Maybe just a ...

"Hi."

She'd spoken quietly but I heard her. I'm sure we all did.

Elise looked at Ronnie. "No, I don't, but if we bought one it would definitely be a purebred. Honestly, though, it's not very tempting." She wrinkled her nose. "Too smelly and dirty."

Ronnie smirked. "Such harsh words for man's best friend."

I snuck a glance at the new lady. She looked unsure what to do. She started to smile at me, but I turned away quickly. Elise sent me a semi-hostile look. Shit. All I did was glance over there.

The new lady cleared her throat and tried again. "Hi."

Ronnie and Elise exchanged a glance that seemed to

mean something. Elise turned toward the new lady. Her eyes swept over her from head to toe. There was an awkward silence.

"Well. I guess you went to Martha's Vineyard this summer." Elise was amazing. She could turn the most harmless words into weapons. With those few words and her cold once-over, she'd made it clear the T-shirt was totally and completely uncool. Not just the T-shirt, but the old jeans, the worn-out Mickey Mouse flip-flops, and the barely brushed hair. Yet she'd done it in a deceptively pleasant voice and with a smile, although not a really warm or fuzzy one. You had to admire that kind of talent. It was a gift, really.

The woman's eyes got wide. She actually started to say, "How did you ..." then stopped when she noticed Elise staring at her chest. It was a "duh" moment. You could almost see her saying to herself, oh that's right, my T-shirt.

There was another awkward silence that must have felt like a century during which time she probably, no definitely, noticed our outfits. Our—if I do say so myself—fashionista-worthy outfits.

"Yes, I ... did," she answered. She was no doubt already wondering just how soon she could get to the mall. And hoping that would help. It wouldn't.

Then another and, if possible, even longer silence was finally broken by the distinctive sound of the approaching school bus. It pulled up, made its farting noise, and spit the kids out. They ran into our waiting arms for comfort, support, and love. Things we gave freely to them. But to everyone else they weren't free. They had to be earned. The hard way.

I looked at Elise. Her daughter chatted a mile a minute about her day, her teacher, her classmates, but Elise was miles away. And I knew. She was planning phase two and beyond. I sighed. I wasn't sure I was ready for another year of this.

RONNIE

Elise was unusually on edge today. With her, it was always about power, but normally she wielded that power subtly. Today the subtlety was gone—practically telling Gail to back off when all she did was ask about Brad. Could there be trouble in paradise?

I poured myself a cup of coffee and sat down at my kitchen table for a brief rest. But I couldn't stop thinking about Elise. I could tell she was annoyed with me, probably because I didn't need to bow down to her highness. Yes, I'd do her bidding, but I didn't have to fawn all over her. I knew Elise lived for the fawning, so the lack of it annoyed her.

She'd started in with the new mom. Hit her with the first of the five "I"s: ignore, insult, intimidate, interrogate, and, finally, if she chose to, initiate. Elise was funny, thinking she was so clever with her important-sounding system of bringing a new member into her inner circle. It was sad to think that to her, this was cleverness. In reality, Elise wasn't nearly as smart or original as she liked to think. This system of hers was just plain bitchiness, dressed up to be something more sophisticated.

I'd noticed something today with the new mom. I was fairly certain I'd seen something in her eyes at the bus stop, some sadness that looked like it wasn't just a reaction to Elise and her "system." The new mom's sadness seemed deeper somehow. But then the look passed. I suppose I might have imagined it.

I doubt any of the others even noticed. Gail and Kelly would be too busy fawning, and Elise, even if she saw her sadness, would misinterpret it. To her it would be merely be a sign her plan was working. It wouldn't occur to her that most people had a life beyond Elise and her carefully designed plans.

Whatever she liked to call this, to me it was getting old. If she insisted on doing this thing, and I knew that she did, then she could at least come up with some new twists. I knew I could, if I were running the show. I knew I could bring true cleverness to the whole process. But of course, that would never happen since I wasn't in charge. And after all, her goals were not my goals. I actually cared far more about other aspects of my life than the role I played in this group.

I couldn't say the same for Elise, though. I often thought this was her whole life. So wrapped up in her game she missed the important stuff like her kids' birthdays and her daughter's music concerts. Yes, she was present at those milestones, but were they really what was important to her? Or was the game more important? The answer was actually kind of sad. But I wouldn't be shedding any tears for her.

Nor for anyone. I had to take care of myself and my kids, which is what I've always done.

Jessie ran in from the family room. "Mommy, we have no homework today. Isn't that terrible?"

I had to laugh. "Jessie, it's the first day of first grade.

Just be patient. You'll get some soon enough."

"Not soon enough for me. I say bring it on."

I laughed again. The girl did me proud, a teacher's pet already in the making. There were worse things to be in my book. I doubted the rhyming girls—Brianna and Diana—were asking about homework.

She opened the pantry door, looking for a snack. "Who's the new girl at the bus stop?"

"Oh, well, she's just a new neighbor." I paused, then tried to get the conversation on safer ground. "I bought you the pudding snacks you like. They're in the refrigerator."

"Brianna said we're not supposed to be her friend."

So much for changing topics. Friendship issues in this group were pretty much a minefield, for both mother and daughter. I really disliked the friendship "games" that went along with this group—I felt the girls were too young to have to deal with clique-related issues. For Pete's sake, that would happen soon enough. But clearly Elise did not share this view.

"Well, Jessie, eventually you might become friends with the new girl. But that takes time. You don't really know her yet. So, it's only natural you wouldn't really talk to her, right now, anyway."

"Oh." She paused, looking serious. "Can I have Doritos instead?"

I laughed with relief since I'd been expecting more friendship discussion. "Yes, fine."

She took a bag out of the cabinet. "But I'm only having, um, what's a serving?"

She had to be kidding. Since when did she care about servings? "I don't know ... why?"

"I'll just have three. Because Brianna says we shouldn't eat junk food."

Oh, how annoying. They were only kids but here was Elise was already brainwashing her daughter—about food, about friends, and who knew what else. These were the obstacles the girls would face on a daily basis. Someday. But not—for Pete's sake—in first grade.

I got out a bowl and added a handful more chips. "Jessie, you're too young and too thin to think like that." I couldn't help adding, "And you're too smart to do everything Brianna says."

I walked away but later I saw the bowl on the counter. The extra chips were still sitting in the bowl, untouched.

BETH

I plopped down on the couch, exhausted both mentally and physically. I was also cold since I hadn't adjusted to the weather here. Even though it wasn't even fall yet, New England weather was always unpredictable, and today felt chilly. I pulled an Ecuadorian blanket, one of several that Rick had brought back from his last trip to his birth country, around my shoulders. Its warmth was comforting. I sighed, rubbing my hands over my eyes.

Rick sat down next to me. "What's wrong, Beth?" He paused. "Is it your mom?"

"Yes. No. I mean ..." What was bothering me? Certainly my mom was never far from my thoughts. But I had to be honest with myself. Right now, that wasn't what was bothering me. I knew Rick wouldn't understand.

Still, I needed to vent, even if he didn't get it. "I think

we made a mistake. Moving here."

"What? Why? You regret being close to your parents? I thought ..."

"No. That's not it. Moving back was the right thing to do. I want my mom to spend time with the kids. While she's able to." My voice broke and I hurried on. "It's just this neighborhood. I don't think we fit in."

"You have to give it time ..."

"Sometimes you just know. Have you seen these yards? All out of a landscaping magazine. And you know how you are. Mowing the lawn once a month. That's not gonna cut it here."

"Beth, I'll mow the lawn every week. Scout's honor." He held up two fingers, but they were the wrong ones. He was making the Hawaiian hang loose sign.

I half-smiled. "You weren't a Scout. And you aren't Hawaiian, either. Although they might think you are. Have you noticed there are no minorities in this neighborhood?" He started to say something but I cut him off, wanting to talk about what was really bothering me. "Anyway, it's more than all that. The women at the bus stop weren't friendly. At all."

"Why do you say that? You know sometimes you ..."

"Don't start." Rick always thought I imagined this kind of thing. But I wasn't imagining it this time. "They didn't even introduce themselves."

"Maybe people in New England don't."

"Rick, I grew up here, remember? And sure, we're not as friendly as Texans, but we still have manners. At least, I thought we did."

"Just because they didn't intro—"

"Rick, they didn't say *anything* to me. Not one word.

They didn't even look my way. Their kids ignored Selena, too."

"It's a two-way street. Maybe you need to—"

"I did. In the afternoon I said hi. Twice before they responded. And all I got for the effort was having my T-shirt made fun of by this gorgeous blonde."

"What did she say?" He paused. "Gorgeous, huh? Maybe I should check out the bus stop." He grinned.

I punched him in the arm but my heart wasn't in it. "She said, 'I guess you went to Martha's Vineyard.'"

He looked confused. "So? You did."

I groaned. "Rick, you don't get it. It was the way she said it. And the way she looked at me."

"Right." He still didn't get it.

"She was obviously saying my T-shirt, actually my whole ... package, was hideous."

"*Caro*, don't worry." His eyes swept the length of me. "I like your whole package." He grinned again. "Later I'll show you just how much. Besides, it's probably just in your—"

"Don't say it." I knew it. I knew he'd think it was in my mind.

He held up his hands. "Okay, okay." He paused. "Don't let it get to you, *Caro*. Who gives a rabbit's ass what they think?"

I couldn't help but smile. He gave me a quick kiss and went out to kick the soccer ball with Ricky.

I ran a hand through my hair. I knew he was probably right. I shouldn't care what they thought of me. Yet, a little voice inside me couldn't help but answer his question. "I do."

CHAPTER TWO

GAIL – THE WANNABE

"Mommy, why do I have to wear this outfit?"

"Because." Once upon a time, I said I'd never answer a child that way. But then, I'd also said I'd never buy Froot Loops. Or let a kid sleep in my bed. But this one bothered me more. I knew kids deserved answers. But I didn't have time for the discussion an answer would bring.

"That's not a reason."

So much for discussion avoidance. I wanted to scream or swear in frustration, but I managed to restrain myself. "Nina, look. Because it's a nice outfit. You want to look pretty, right?"

"Daddy says I always look pretty."

"Of course you do, sweetie." Freaking Joe. Thanks a lot.

"Then ... it doesn't matter what I wear."

Grrr. "Look. It just ... it matters. Okay?" It so mattered. She had no idea how much.

"I want to wear my jeans."

"Those jeans with the holes? And not even fashionable holes, they're just holey because they're falling apart. No. Absolutely not."

"Mommy, please?"

"Look, wear the outfit I picked for you and you can watch *Marly* when you get home."

She considered. I was sure I had her.

"And *Johnny and Max*." Her voice was firm. Damn. She'd make a great lawyer.

"Deal. Now go. Hurry."

She ran off to change and I thought of Elise. I was sure she didn't have to go through this let's-make-a-deal business. Or Kelly since she was practically Elise's twin. And definitely not Ronnie. Her kids would never dare disobey her. I sometimes wondered what her secret was, since outwardly she seemed mild and harmless. But I noticed her kids listened to her and never talked back.

So, I was pretty sure it was just me. The sole lousy parent. Or maybe not. The new mom on the block, from the looks of things, might give me a run for my money. She could potentially steal the title from me. The title of most likely to never win Mother of the Year.

Somehow, we made it out the door five minutes later. But as I pulled up to the stop, they were all there already. Well, I thought with relief, at least there was someone now who was worse than me. She was MIA as of now. I hoped it would take her a while to figure out the rules. So I'd have more time to bask in the glow of not being the lowest of the low.

ELISE – THE QUEEN BEE

Kelly smirked. "Check out Gail's little girl. Trying way too hard, per usual."

I chuckled. "Well, that's our Gail. She makes trying too hard an art form."

I glanced over my shoulder to see her latest attempt, and saw that, yes, Nina was dressed to impress. But although I'd just agreed with Kelly, secretly I had to hand it to Gail. She certainly did not get everything right, but when it came to fashion the woman had some chops. In all honesty, Kelly could learn a thing or two from her.

And, clearly, she already had her eyes on best dressed for her daughter. Being the generous woman that I was, I'd let her have that. She was deserving, after all. Gail had paid her dues. And she'd keep on paying.

"Hi, Gail." I paused and Kelly and Ronnie issued similar greetings. I pretended to notice Nina's outfit for the first time. "Nina, honey, you look amazing."

"Thank you, Miss Dresden." She ran off to play with the others.

I caught Gail cringing. She knew I liked the kids to call me Elise. Still, I thought it was cute how her daughter called me Miss. It made me sound young. Well, I was young. But I liked to be reminded of that fact. At my smile, Gail relaxed.

"Gail, I can already predict the other girls will be looking to Nina for fashion advice."

Gail's face broke into a huge smile. I couldn't resist asking the next question, though. "Did you get rid of her horrible pair of jeans?"

The smile disappeared. "Um, I'm working on it."

"Well. Kids can be so ... challenging. Just today Brianna insisted on eating Brad's Froot Loops. But I had to put my foot down. I had to tell her Froot Loops are not acceptable breakfast food." A little white lie. Brianna hated Froot Loops. I did hide Brad's stash, mainly so Jordan wouldn't find them.

Gail nodded her head so hard her earrings shook. I snuck a glance at Ronnie and caught her smirk, ever so slightly. Gail clearly gave her kid Froot Loops. I suppressed a grin. "So, what does Nina like for breakfast?"

She chewed on a nail then glanced at the others. They

were silent. "Well, she likes oatmeal."

Right. And Brad's joining the clergy.

Suddenly Gail said, "Look. Isn't that the new lady?" She sounded a bit desperate.

I turned to look. I started to say, "I don't see ..." but then I trailed off. A gray minivan was approaching us. Actually a minivan. I knew this woman had no taste, I mean that oversized T-shirt was ... well, words can't describe how bad ... but the husband must have no taste either to pick a car like that. And a wife like that.

Maybe that last thought was beneath me. Or maybe not.

After all, someone had to uphold the standards of the neighborhood. We were the best 'hood in town and, as such, we had an image to keep. This new woman needed to know that. Like clay, she could be molded into the type of mom worthy of our street. Maybe. As I watched her pull to the curb, I wondered whether such a transformation was possible. Maybe yes, maybe no. That remained to be seen. But regardless, she did need to know her place. That was nonnegotiable.

RONNIE – THE INFORMER

I watched Nina step out of Gail's car, looking like she was ready for a photo shoot. Cue the cameras, I felt like yelling. Where was the American Girl team to film this young child in all her glorious fashion perfection?

Obviously, I knew what this meant—the race for best dressed was on. The gauntlet had been thrown. But, luckily for Gail, that was a category I didn't care about. I suspected Elise would concede in that area as well. Kelly had been somewhat of an unknown; I wondered if maybe Elise had her heart set on best dressed for her sidekick, but her words proved otherwise. And Kelly would go along with whatever Elise decided.

It wasn't surprising she had conceded. Elise would have her eye on best looking or most popular—the glam categories—and any leftovers would go to Kelly's daughter. Gail had chosen well. I looked at her with fresh eyes. Maybe she was smarter than I'd given her credit for. I'd need to watch her more closely in the future.

As for my daughter, I was more than okay with smartest. The other categories would be nice, but they were hardly necessary. My daughter would use her brain— I prayed not in the way I had—and she would accomplish much in her life.

I watched the new mom sit in her car, trying to work up the nerve to get out. We had that effect on people. I knew of at least one mom in this neighborhood who had started to drive her kids to school, basically admitting she wasn't in our league. There were some families who had switched to other bus stops. Those were the weak ones. I had little sympathy for them. They should have stayed and dealt with us. But it was their loss since there would be no reward for them.

New Mom's car door opened. She got out and walked over to us while holding her daughter's hand. The daughter was cute. Not that anyone here would ever tell her that.

I noticed the mom's outfit right away, as did the others I'm sure. She'd dressed up since yesterday, but she was far from where she needed to be. Her T-shirt was gone;

instead she had on a blouse and Capris, but the pants were too tight and ... oh, wait. They weren't Capris; they were just too-short pants masquerading as Capris.

I glanced at Elise and knew she'd seen. I felt an unusual stab of ... what appeared to be actual pity for the woman. Get thee to a mall, I would've said, if I was feeling generous, but then, I rarely was.

Sure enough, as the new mom walked over, Elise did her thing: the cold once-over. But this time she did not speak to the woman. Instead she turned to me, speaking in a clearly audible voice. "You know, I always forget. What length are Capri pants supposed to be?"

So obvious. But I played along. "Mid-calf."

"Oh. Right." She paused as if considering that. "Then, I guess ..." here she broke off to stare at New Mom's calves, then continued, "... anything longer must be ..." she trailed off.

"High waters," Gail supplied, as if shouting out the answer in a game of Trivial Pursuit. Elise never did the dirty work. Saying the offending word was someone else's job.

"Right," I answered, imagining I was a game show host. "That is correct." I almost added, "Tell the lady what she's won."

I turned to glance at New Mom in time to see her cheeks turn pink. Oddly though, it became her. I suddenly realized she was pretty. I wasn't sure how old she was exactly but for having a teenage son, she looked young. She did have a little bit of fat, probably from the baby, at her middle, but other than that she was surprisingly attractive. Yes, she did need some improvements in fashion and the way she carried herself, but she definitely had more going for her than Elise would want to admit.

None of that mattered, of course. Being pretty wouldn't help her; Elise would just hate her all the more for it.

Before I turned back to the group, I rolled my eyes slightly, which was intended for New Mom only. I looked back at Elise checking to make sure she hadn't seen but I was fine. She was busy sharing a look with Kelly.

The kids got on the bus. We ignored New Mom and she didn't attempt to speak to us. I suspected she wanted to run home in shame, but she squared her shoulders and walked calmly to her car. I had to give her credit; she didn't really show that we'd bothered her. There was no sign we'd gotten to her other than the color of her cheeks. When she drove off, I caught a glimpse of the car seat in the back. She must have figured out having the baby in her arms wouldn't help get her noticed. She was right about that at least.

Gail said, "We did good, right?"

Elise looked annoyed. She didn't like to have obvious questions asked. She wouldn't dignify that with an answer.

Kelly would, though—in fact, that was her job. "We did great. Didn't you see her face? The woman looked shell-shocked."

Gail looked embarrassed. "I definitely noticed her pink face."

Elise couldn't restrain herself anymore. "Pink? More like indigo. Or maybe violet."

"ROY G BIV." They all stared blankly at me. "Hello? The colors of the spectrum?" I got the same blank stare. Honestly, was I the only one here who paid attention in science class? I sighed. "Anyway, whatever color you choose, it became her."

Now everyone looked at me like I had three heads. I put on my innocent look. "What? I'm just saying the woman is pretty." I knew this would tick Elise off, but I said it anyway. I gave myself a mental pat on the back.

True to form, she said, "Pretty? You mean pretty ... ugly."

This was an old joke with this group. We would look at a woman and one of us would say, "Oh, she's pretty." Then someone else would add, "Pretty ugly."

"The woman's not ugly." I might be pressing it, but I couldn't help myself.

Elise glared at me. Her glare had some serious bite to it; in fact, there'd been a time when it could make me, if not tremble, then at least fidget. But, as the awkward silence continued, I realized, with a sickening feeling, I wasn't totally immune, even now.

"Look. I'm not saying she's beautiful, for Pete's sake. And clearly, the woman needs fashion help." There. That would no doubt placate her.

Sure enough, the glare disappeared. "Fashion ... help?" She snorted. She was the only woman I knew who could make a snort sound classy. "More like call in the fashion police for an emergency meeting. Not that they could even help."

The group talked more about fashion, but my thoughts wandered. I found fashion boring, in truth I guess I always had, even back in high school. I'd always suspected the popular crowd cared way too much about such unimportant matters and judging from my experience with this group of women, I'd been right. I did buy the "right" clothes from the "right" stores, because I had to, but in truth I couldn't care less. Finally, we went our separate ways, which was the best part of the morning. They were my ... friends, I guess you could say, but for some reason it was the same every day. I always couldn't wait to leave.

BETH – THE TARGET

Last Friday I had made a total shamble of my room and my closet, trying in vain to find decent clothes. Bus stop-worthy clothes—how ridiculous was that? But it was no use. I had all this stuff, yet somehow nothing I could wear. Not with this critical group—this unbelievably mean and critical group.

So, yesterday I'd given in and gone to the mall. Rick even approved. For a straight guy, he was into shopping in a scary way. I hadn't told him about the reason I needed clothes. I knew I'd just get another speech from him, along with another bunch of questions. Like, why the hell do you care? And, who gives some kind of animal's ass? I didn't want to think about those questions. Maybe because I had no good answers.

But I couldn't help thinking for the millionth time, *What the heck is with these women?* After talking to Rick the other day, I was willing to believe he might have been right. Maybe that T-shirt incident had been in my mind. Maybe, although I doubted it, the blonde really had been just making conversation. But not the most recent assault. No, it was definitely not in my mind. These women were cruel. The whole thing was so unusual. I couldn't even remember high school being this bad.

They just seemed like such a united front. All together in their seeming dislike of me. But just what had I done to deserve that? What cardinal sin had I committed? Other than being totally fashionless?

I stared at my new clothes laid out on my bed. Would they even help? And wasn't it silly to give in to these fashion-crazy women just to fit in? Well, at least now I wouldn't be quite so fashionless.

"Mommy, come tuck me in," Selena called from her room.

Hearing Selena made me wonder: Were their daughters being mean to her too? I didn't think so. I thought in her case they were just ignoring her. They better not start on her, too, I thought. If they did, there'd be hell to pay. I might not stick up for myself, but I'd stick up for her. Someway, somehow, I would.

I went to her room and gathered the covers around her. As if reading my thoughts, Selena suddenly asked, "Are you going to walk me over in the morning?"

"Do you want to walk over by yourself?" Even armed with my new fashions, it was too tempting not to ask. But I already knew the answer.

"Nooo," she whined, "I want you to come with me."

I kissed her. "Okay, I will." I tried not to cringe. "It's a school night, so get some sleep."

I started walking out, but for some reason her Disney princess lamp caught my eye. I always loved that lamp. Disney was one of my favorite places and the lamp reminded me of many happy vacations. The princesses were so pretty and the artwork on the lamp so well done. I found myself looking at Cinderella, who was facing me.

Suddenly, I realized why she'd caught my eye. The blond at the bus stop looked just like Cinderella—same color and length of hair, almost the same hairstyle, and the same perfect features. After coming to this realization, the lamp lost some of its appeal.

I started out of the room but then I couldn't help it. I walked back and turned the lamp so that Belle was facing out. I had always liked Belle better anyway. She likes to read and could actually fall in love with a beast. Yes, she was my kind of princess.

"Why'd you turn the lamp?" Selena asked.

"Oh, well ... if you don't rotate the lamp then one princess always gets to look out. I thought Belle might want a turn."

Selena laughed at my silly answer as I left the room. I couldn't very well tell her the truth.

Luckily, the baby was already asleep so I would have a little time to read. As I lay down with my book, I remembered that once, when Selena was younger, she kept taking toys out of her cousin's hand. She was really into princesses at the time and insisted Tobey call her Cinderella.

I remembered him whining, "She's a mean Cinderella."

But now I suspected I'd discovered a far meaner one.

CHAPTER THREE

THE TARGET

I woke up late. The alarm never went off. Somehow I managed to get everybody ready and we rushed out the door. But in the car I realized the baby was only wearing a diaper. Selena yelled from the back, "Mommy, you're going to bring the baby out like that?" But I couldn't turn around. Selena would be late. At the bus stop I tried to get Selena to walk over by herself, but she started whining.

I got out of the car, suddenly realizing I was wearing a Belle costume. Where were my new clothes? I was mortified until I realized the blonde was dressed in a Cinderella gown. I thought, *Wow, maybe today I'll fit in.* But my hopes were soon dashed.

The blonde looked me over and sneered, "I'm the only princess here."

"Wait until midnight," I said. "Then we'll see who's the real princess."

She raised her perfectly arched eyebrows in surprise, just as the clock started striking midnight. Suddenly her beautiful gown began turning into rags, as she watched in horror. She ran toward me but tripped on her glass slippers, and fell, pulling at my gown ...

I woke up to Rick shoving my shoulder to shut off the alarm. I reached over and killed the beeping as it sunk in that the whole thing had been a dream. I should have known; I never delivered witty comebacks.

In real time, I got myself and the kids ready, and we headed out early, or so I thought. But as I drove down the street, I saw they were all there already. The real-life Stepford wives. I parked and walked over, hoping against hope my new clothes would provide some sort of miracle cure. But I soon saw nothing had changed. No one even looked my way. They were deep into their little circle. Unbelievable. Hundreds of bucks in debt—for nothing.

Realizing I'd given in to their peer pressure, and so easily, made me feel silly. Even ashamed. I was an adult now. So, why had I taken the bait? I could've kept wearing my old clothes that were, more or less, fine. But their pointed dissing of my subpar clothes—and, by extension, my sense of style and how I chose to present myself—had activated something in me. Some old, yet still present, longing to be accepted. To fit in. Throughout middle school and high school, this had always been my desire, yet it remained unattainable.

With this old pain reactivated, I felt tears ready to fall but I managed to blink them back. I was being stupid and silly, I knew. Why did I even care? Wasn't I beyond this? These women weren't worth a second thought, never mind tears.

I pulled myself out of my self-pity party when I noticed their daughters. They were also in a tight circle formation—gee, where did they learn that?—and my daughter was, no surprise, also excluded. The girls were playing a simple game of catch. My daughter stood next to one of the girls, eyeing the game with a look a blind man could have read.

But again, and no surprise, the girls totally ignored her. Suddenly I felt fury. Their mothers could treat me like shit, but I'd be damned if they'd do it to my daughter. After all, I wasn't a kid anymore. I didn't have to be the quiet doormat from high school who would take whatever crap the popular people dished out. No, I was an adult now. I could do something about it.

But, despite my tough inner talk, I hesitated. I noticed the mothers' avoidance of me seemed to apply to their kids too. They were laughing and talking, totally oblivious to the girls' game. That was good.

So, I made my move. I knew who the girls' leader was. Even if it hadn't been obvious by the color of her hair and the resemblance to her mother, I could tell. The girl radiated a confidence I had to admire.

But, I reminded myself again, I was the adult here. I took a few steps and stood next to her. She ignored me, too. A quick glance at the moms told me they were still not paying any attention to me or them.

I cleared my throat. "My daughter would like to play." I struggled to speak calmly. I was mad, but I knew anger wouldn't help.

The girl turned toward me with a surprised and innocent look. She was good, but I wasn't fooled. "Oh, I'm sorry," she said. "I didn't see her." She was obviously lying since there was no way she could've not seen us, yet she'd spoken in such a believable voice. I wouldn't have thought it possible for a young girl to pull off deceit so well.

But two of the girls moved over, giving my daughter room to join their game. As I stepped back, I couldn't help sneaking another glance at the moms. The coast was clear. I sighed with relief. I hated confrontations.

My eyes went back to the girls. The ball was tossed around several times, yet no one threw it to my daughter. This went on for a minute or two. The ball continued to be passed to every girl but Selena. I shook my head in frustration. These girls were something else. I was about to speak up again, when the blonde girl suddenly aimed the ball right at my daughter. But now, instead of a friendly game, it looked like my daughter was the target in a nasty game of dodgeball. A look of equal parts confusion and fear crossed Selena's face. At that exact moment the bus pulled around the corner.

The blonde girl dropped the ball. She glanced in my direction and shrugged. "Sorry. Game over." She turned to take her usual place in line—first—but not before I caught the smirk on her face.

Great. I'd spoken up but what had it accomplished? Nothing. Selena never even got to touch the ball. And then she'd almost been pelted with it.

Something made me look over at the moms. The blonde was staring at me, her expression a replica of her daughter's. Suddenly, I knew. She'd seen the whole thing. Somehow, some way. Did the woman have eyes in the back of her head? Maybe she wasn't human. That could explain a lot, actually.

THE QUEEN BEE

"Well, the woman's got some balls," Ronnie said, as she watched New Mom drive off. I thought I detected some admiration in her voice.

I had to quell that. "Because she speaks up to a bunch of first graders?"

Ronnie only shrugged.

Kelly was quick with backup, as always. "Yeah, right. That really makes her eligible for a bravery award." She laughed at her own comment while Gail giggled along.

Ronnie said, "Still. She did do something."

I nodded slowly. "Well, she's not exactly going to set the world on fire with her toughness, but yes, she did something. And that can't be neglected."

Kelly and Gail both got the look in their eyes—excitement and curiosity mixed with a dose of fear. I always loved that look.

Ronnie's expression didn't change. The woman had on her poker face. It was maddening sometimes but then it was one of the things that made her such an important ally.

"So, we need a plan." I gave Ronnie a significant look. Sometimes I made the plans myself but sometimes I let my subordinates handle things. I liked to delegate when possible; it meant my hands were clean. Cleaner, anyway.

Ronnie nodded and said, "No problem." Her face gave away nothing. But I knew I could count on her. I didn't choose my lieutenants lightly.

"I'll need to know when everything's in place." I glanced at Kelly and Gail. Then at Ronnie again. I knew she would understand what the looks meant. I was simply reminding her I didn't want the others to know the plan. I liked them to be surprised as well. It was part of the fun.

Ronnie nodded again. "Copy that."

I gave her a funny look, but then when I understood, I almost grinned. Ronnie was too funny. Yes, she understood her place. Without my ever having to say it.

We went our separate ways then. For me this was the dullest part of the day. How to spend the next few hours? I could go shopping. Again. But I didn't really need anything. Or I could think about what to make for dinner.

Maybe attempt some gourmet meal to impress Brad. But he wasn't exactly a foodie type.

At least I didn't have to worry about housework. Fancy Maids were coming this morning, a company Brad found online. The maids actually wore the French maid outfit— not the boring uniform but the actual Halloween-like costume that almost looks like what a stripper would wear—when they showed up to clean. Remembering this, I decided I'd better hang around and keep Brad honest. Maybe entertained as well. Not that I didn't trust him. It's just the guy had a huge appetite, in so many ways.

THE WANNABE

I pulled the car up to the curb for afternoon pickup and was greeted by a sight that made my pulse speed up. Brad was here. And even better, Elise wasn't. The only downside was both Kelly and Ronnie were already there. If I'd known Brad would be here, and alone, I would've been early—I mean really early. But we never knew when he'd show. He was one of life's pleasant surprises.

I knew I shouldn't care one way or the other. I was a married woman. He was a married man. And not to just anyone. He was the better half—literally—to the best-looking woman in the neighborhood, if not the whole town. But more important was her influence. You didn't want to be on her bad side. No. I had nightmares just thinking about that.

But whenever I saw him, I couldn't help it. My body reacted before my brain. As long as my thoughts stayed in my brain, I believed I was safe. At least I hoped so.

I walked over. He noticed me right away with a smile. "Hey, Gail." Elise never acknowledged me that soon. Another reason I liked him.

"Hi, Brad." I smiled back, hoping I didn't look too eager.

His eyes swept over me. "Lookin' good."

I felt my cheeks get warm. Look, it was no big deal, I told myself. If he said that in front of the others, clearly it was just a little harmless flirtation.

"Thanks," I managed, then snuck a look at Ronnie. She was eying me with that way of hers. Like she could read my thoughts.

Brad looked like he forgot something. "You ladies aren't too shabby either," he said, looking in turn at Kelly and Ronnie. Kelly smiled, looking flattered. Even Ronnie looked like she was fighting a smile. I guess even she wasn't immune to Brad's charms.

Kelly asked, "Where's Elise?"

"She went to get her hair done. Or maybe it was nails." He grinned. "I don't know. Someone's working on something of hers."

Kelly said quickly, "Not that she needs any work." The woman was so loyal, even when Elise was absent. I wasn't sure if that was nice or just plain sick.

Brad stared at Kelly. "Right." I could tell he didn't like her correcting him. But he soon shrugged it off. "So. You ladies coming to the end-of-summer fling?"

Oh shit. I'd forgotten about that. Elise and Brad always threw an end-of-summer party one of the weekends in September. It was informal, no invitations. But it was mandatory attendance. I didn't mind going, exactly, it was just that I wasn't in the best bathing-suit shape. I had managed to gain a few pounds over the summer. Later, I'd go buy some laxatives, my secret weight loss weapon.

I noticed the others had all nodded or said yes. Brad was looking at me, waiting. I managed a nod. He smiled and again my pulse quickened.

Just then we heard a car pull up. Brad looked over but the rest of us didn't need to. We knew who it was.

"Who's that?" Brad asked.

Did Elise tell him nothing? I glanced at the other two and kept my mouth shut. I'd let someone else handle this.

"It's just the new mom in the 'hood," Ronnie supplied. She gave Kelly and me a significant look, but I didn't really know what she meant. I wasn't good at nonverbal communication. In fact, sometimes it was like Ronnie and Elise were on some kind of mental highway only they could reach.

"Why isn't she getting out of her car?" Brad asked.

Duh. Because we scare the shit out of her. And we're good at it. True, most of the credit didn't go to me, but still, I was a card-carrying member of this group. Elise actually had cards made.

Kelly and I looked at Ronnie, who seemed to be our momentary de facto leader. "I don't know." Ronnie shrugged, looking unconcerned. "Maybe she's listening to some tunes."

"Or maybe the baby's crying," Kelly said.

"Or maybe she's painting her toenails," I said. They all looked at me funny. "What? I paint my toes in the car."

Ronnie smirked. "Yeah. While you're driving."

Brad grinned. "Gail, I didn't know you were so talented."

I could feel myself blush. "I don't ..."

But Brad talked over me. "Anyway. I think you're all wrong. A, I hear no music. B, I hear no crying and C," he looked at me, "she would either be bending over to reach her toes or we'd see her feet."

"A sight you don't want to see." Ronnie was still smirking. "Trust me."

"Yeah. No expensive pedicures for her," Kelly said.

I glanced at my feet. Thank goodness I had on closed-toe shoes.

The sound of the approaching school bus could be heard before the big yellow thing appeared. The car door opened, and New Mom got out. We all stared at her feet. No nail polish. Brad and I exchanged a glance.

The kids ran over to their respective parents and New Mom got right back in. She was in a rush, actually peeling out as she drove off. It was a hastier exit than I'd ever seen her make. Something must have scared her this time more than ever. I wondered what it was. If I knew, I could have some dirt to impress Elise with.

Ronnie was staring after New Mom with a curious expression. Shit, she'd noticed too. I knew my chances of finding anything out paled in comparison to Ronnie's abilities. She always seemed to know more than the rest of us. It was kind of scary. But nowhere near as scary as Elise's, er, ... scariness.

KELLY – THE SIDEKICK

Diana was in front of the TV watching her afternoon show, some sliced apples by her side. They were a healthy snack that Elise, and Brianna, both approved of. Yes, snacks should be healthy, but I'd thought an occasional treat was okay. But Elise strongly disagreed when we discussed this the other day, so I backpedaled. She was probably right. You couldn't be too careful with what you allowed your kids to eat.

I went into the small alcove in the family room and pulled out my desk. When it was closed it looked like a small coffee table. But it was actually where I did my insurance job every afternoon. Elise, and the others, knew nothing about it. I didn't even tell Diana, because I was afraid she'd spill my secret. Elise felt strongly that mothers shouldn't work. But it was so easy for her—Brad made lots of money and got to work from home, too; how unfair was that? My husband was a cop, a lowly paid and dangerous occupation. Well, not that dangerous in our town, but still. And Elise with her always wanting to go get her nails done or facials or what have you—I had to pay for that somehow. I don't know how she thought I managed it. Maybe she thought Steve had a side job. Or worse, that he was doing something illegal. I knew he did, very occasionally, smoke pot with Brad, but that was legal after all in some places now, although not Connecticut. Other than that, he was a straight-up honest person. Truthfully, I suspected Elise was just a little clueless about how much cops made. Most people were.

My job was a necessary evil; we needed the money, but it was so uncool. I knew that if Elise knew she would not only hate that I was working but hate that the job itself was so ... pedestrian. I felt trapped though. What other job could I get? Working at McDonald's? At least with this I could work from home and keep it secret. I worked for a successful agent, Blair Landon, in another town, so my name wasn't on any of the advertising. I even answered the phone as Kelly-Ann, which I thought of as my alter ego—an extremely lame one. Although I did sometimes worry about the truth coming out, oddly, I felt pretty secure in my ability to be sneaky.

I'd read somewhere that when people give up the idea of doing what they love, they start selling insurance. Well, maybe that was true. Maybe I had given up. Maybe this was all there was for me, all I deserved career-wise.

At least today I didn't have to make phone calls, I just had to do paperwork. I hated the cold calling and being hung up on; it was like constant rejection. Or like a validation that what I had to say wasn't important.

While I did the mindless work, my mind went back to the bus stop this afternoon. Brad had been there today. Without Elise. I didn't get it. Why did she send him there alone? It was like she sent the big bad wolf to hang out with the three little pigs. Not that we resemble pigs. Although Gail did look like she'd put on a pound or two.

Brad had just flirted so much. Steve could be a flirt, sometimes. But not like Brad. I mean giving us the once-over? Saying we look good? I didn't think that was cool. Although it had been kind of nice to hear. I guess I still "got it." Even though Steve didn't say that stuff to me anymore.

Brad's looks were the problem—he was just too good looking. He could get women so easily. Probably lots of women. In fact, it really wouldn't have surprised me if he'd... no, I wouldn't go there. It felt too disloyal to even think like that. Anyway, Elise could handle anything thrown her way, any problem. She was always in control.

As her number one, I would continue to do what I could to remind her husband of what he has. Elise was not someone to take lightly.

I hoped Elise appreciated what I do for her. I was the only one who truly looked out for her. The rest only did it for their own personal reasons. I did it because ... well, because I care. Because of our strong friendship. What's more, I knew that I could tell her anything. Well, not everything, I mean not about my job. But most everything else. And she knew she can tell me anything too. She didn't really confide in me much, but I'm here for her, like always.

Actually, I was pretty sure Elise did appreciate me. It was not her style to say thanks or get all mushy or sentimental, but then who needs that anyway? I knew she doesn't believe in apologizing either, to her it's a sign of weakness. She hated it when some women go around always saying sorry for this, sorry for that. I knew she thinks men don't apologize much, so why should women? Which was actually kind of feminist.

Then, too, I guess if you think you're always right, there's no need to apologize.

THE INFORMER

I got dinner on the table, and the kids out of their rooms for our family dinner. I knew that it's supposed to be family time, a time for being together and actually talking to each other rather than staring at our phones or other devices. But even though I believed having family time is important, my mind was miles away. All I could think about was the plan. I needed a plan. I knew I could come up with something, in my sleep if necessary. But I wanted it to be more than good. I was going for greatness. I wanted to show off my superior skills. If I was going to do this thing, I'd do it to the best of my ability. That was my nature after all.

I knew that patience was part of the game. If I rushed, the result wouldn't be as good. I needed to lie in wait, sort of like a serial killer. And wait for the right time to strike.

Part of waiting involved gathering facts about the target. Like today, New Mom had blitzed out of there like never before. Why? What was different today? Oh, right, it was so obvious. Brad was the difference. With this realization, I almost shouted out loud.

I caught Ian looking at me quizzically. "You alright, hon?"

"Yes." I smiled, without even having to force it. "I'm fine." I was better than fine, actually. Now I had another puzzle piece. But what was it about Brad? Why had he freaked her out?

It was unlikely that just the sight of an incredibly good-looking guy would send her running in the other direction. Although, I did remember a time in my distant past when I thought good-looking guys were kind of scary. But even then, I wouldn't have run from them. Usually, they were the ones doing the running.

I sent that negative thought packing. I wasn't a total loser in school. In my group of the smart ones, I'd hardly been the lowest. True, kids in other higher cliques called us nerds but we weren't. We knew we were better than them. Smarter. We were the ones who would go far in life, while they were the ones who would live the rest of their lives trying to relive their glory days. Despite knowing I had the upper hand in many ways, I had to admit that I'd been far from where the truly hot guys hung out back then—the top of the food chain.

Anyway, now I was making up for all that, big time. I had achieved a lot in the way of social status since those days. I'd paid my dues in high school but was reaping the rewards now.

But even better than my social status was my daughter's. I was buying a place for her in her social realm, a place far higher than the one I occupied. A coveted place, where she and her friends would reign supreme. I hoped someday she'd understand what I did for her. And if not thank me, then at the very least, not condemn me.

Enough with these runaway thoughts, I told myself. Concentrate. Why had Brad scared New Mom?

Ian cleared his throat, eyeing me with a worried expression. Okay, point taken. This would have to wait. Hadn't I just the other day accused Elise of ignoring her family because of the game? I wasn't that far gone. I wasn't—God forbid—as bad as her.

I forced myself into the here and now. "Jessie, did you finish your homework?"

She rolled her eyes. "Mommy. I did it right when I got home."

"Oh. Well ... good." I was happy she did it so soon but what was with the eye roll? Wasn't that a teen thing? Or a moms-who-act-like-teens thing, like the moms at the bus stop? "Anyway, you must be happy to have homework finally."

"It was only one paper. I asked for more, but Mrs. Long said that was it for today."

"Believe it or not, Jessie, there'll come a day when you won't want homework." I wasn't sure why I said that, except that it was inevitable. Sad, but inevitable.

She looked at me with wide eyes. "I hope not."

I laughed. But when she looked away, I said quietly, "Me too."

Nick piped up. "Mom, just so you know? I'm already there."

I couldn't help but laugh again. Because I knew Nick was a good kid. He might complain but he did his work. My kids were not slackers. I made sure of that.

CHAPTER FOUR

THE TARGET

I lay down on my bed but sleep wouldn't come. I couldn't believe my bad luck. I mean first I find out the neighborhood moms were like some twisted mafia enforcing ... what? Good fashion? And then I'd bought new expensive clothes, but it hadn't changed a thing. Clearly they were enforcing more than fashion. Just what, I still had no clue.

As if that wasn't bad enough, then I recognized one of their husbands. And I'd put money on whom he belonged to. The guy who looked like Prince Charming—appropriately from *Shrek*, not the Disney movie—must be Cinderella's husband. It was just too perfect.

At first I didn't remember his name. But it came back to me later as I walked down a mental memory lane from high school. Brad was popular, cool, and good looking even then, and apparently not much had changed. He'd been in a totally different social class than me. Probably he didn't remember me, since he hadn't even noticed my existence back then. But, either way, just the sight of him made me want to hurl. I'm sure that wasn't the usual response he got from the ladies, especially judging by the way the other moms were looking at him.

But seeing a familiar face from school reminded me of one of the reasons I'd moved away after graduating. I'd wanted to go far away and start fresh, somewhere no one knew me. Somewhere I could be anything or anyone. But I'd found it wasn't so easy. The box you were put into in high school? Well, mine must have been locked. And the key thrown far away.

Even so, time had changed me, at least a little. I had more confidence now; I was more comfortable with myself. But when I saw someone from that time of my life—especially someone high and mighty like Brad—it was like I was suddenly thrown back in time against my will. And I became that mousy little girl once again, that nobody I'd been in high school.

"*Caro*, what's the matter?"

I looked up, startled to see Rick standing in the bedroom doorway, looking at me with concern. "Nothing," I managed. I sat up and tried to smile but didn't quite make it.

"Didn't look like nothing to me."

I hesitated but then decided to try an idea I had. "Rick. The women at the bus stop? They're still being ... bitchy." Even that word barely covered it. But since I feared a speech about how it was "in my mind," I went on quickly, "Especially Cinderella. She's the ringleader."

Rick had started to say, "Beth, maybe ..." He stopped, looking confused. "What ... who's Cinderella?"

"Only the meanest Cinderella I've ever seen." I paused. "Not that I've seen a lot of them."

"Are you feeling okay?" He looked concerned. Clearly, I was confusing him. At least he had forgotten his speech.

"And then Prince Charming shows up today. It was just so perfect. In an extremely sick and horrible way."

"Prince Charming? Um, Beth, who exactly are these people at the bus stop? Are they all named after fairy tale people?"

"Yeah." I couldn't help teasing him. "There's a

Goldilocks and a Little Red Riding Hood too." He just looked at me like I'd gone off the deep end. So, I went on quickly, "Look, Rick, two of them remind me of Cinderella and Charming. Anyway, that's not the point. The point is I think I'm gonna start driving Selena to school."

"What? That's crazy. It's just more work for you. And anyway, the bus is a good way for Selena to make friends."

I couldn't help rolling my eyes. "Yeah, that's working real well so far."

"You have to give it time. Maybe you aren't trying hard enough. Both of you."

"Oh? Then, I guess you could do better?"

"Yeah. I probably could."

"Good. Prove it."

"What?"

"Go to the bus stop tomorrow."

He shook his head. "I have to work, *Caro*, you know that."

"Just go in late. One day. Just to ... show me how much better you are."

"Beth, I can't." He grinned. "I'll show you how good I am, right now if you want."

I rolled my eyes, again. *Guys.* "That's not what I mean. Anyway, if you won't go tomorrow then that's it. I'm driving her."

He raised his eyebrows. "I guess you mean business."

"Yes. I do." I was determined to stand my ground on this.

He ran his hand through his hair but was silent.

I sighed with relief. It looked like I'd managed to solve my bus stop problems, since I wanted to start driving her.

Rick suddenly said, "Okay. You win. I'll go with you

tomorrow."

I sighed again, this time from annoyance. Great. I won. So why didn't I feel victorious?

THE QUEEN BEE

"Well, I hate to repeat myself, but now it's even more appropriate. Guess who's coming to dinner this time?" Ronnie smirked.

I followed her glance and saw what she meant. New Mom was parking her car. But she had her husband with her. The first thing I noticed was he was kind of cute—if you could go for his darker, more mysterious look—which I didn't. Brad was like a blond, blue-eyed surfer dude. Although he didn't surf, he fit that profile. New Dad fit another kind of profile. One that would get him stopped at airports.

I had to hand it to New Mom. She was already calling in for reinforcements. It was a smart tactical move, even if I had a perfect counter move. I always did. Yet, it made me think that, perhaps, she could be worthy of our group. Someday. After much humbling and groveling.

She and her husband stopped a little short of our circle. New Mom was saying something to her husband, at which he shook his head.

He cleared his throat. "Good morning, ladies."

Ronnie and I exchanged a glance that passed for words. I turned toward him, smiling my brightest smile. I pushed my hair back from my shoulder. I knew that move always showed off my perfect biceps. Sure enough, he noticed. "Good morning. Lovely day, isn't it?"

"Yeah, it's like summer today."

"Yes, it should be nice for a few more weeks."

He shared a glance with his wife. She looked confused. I planned to make that intensify.

"I'm Elise." I took two steps over to them and held out my hand, smiling.

"Nice to meet you. I'm Rick." He smiled back and indicated his wife. "And this is my wife, Beth."

I turned to her, shook her hand, and smiled again, but this time it wasn't my friendly one. I knew she could tell the difference. The husband would be clueless, however.

"Hello." From her one word I knew she still didn't trust us, and, well, she shouldn't, but she was slightly hopeful. Which was a change from yesterday.

"I know we've spoken before, but I forgot to introduce myself."

"Oh. That's okay." An unreadable look passed over her face.

Ronnie and the others had followed me over. They all introduced themselves. Ronnie—the great actress that she was—actually complimented the baby Beth had in her arms. How Ronnie managed the compliment with a straight face was beyond me. The kid had this lock of jet-black hair that stood straight up, somehow defying gravity. Did they gel it into place or something?

We chatted and the bus came; the kids boarded and left. As the couple walked back to their car, they seemed to be discussing something. I would love to have been a fly in their car on the way back. Well, not a fly because they're so dirty and ugly. Maybe a crystal hanging from the rearview mirror. Anyway, I knew New Mom, or Beth, would be wondering what to think, wondering why we had been suddenly nice. And her husband would now never believe we'd been anything but. It was a great performance. Ronnie and I should give theatre a try. Except I was pretty sure this was much more fun. After all, who needed the fake atmosphere of theatre? The real world was my stage.

THE WANNABE

I pulled up that afternoon, and what do you know? Two days in a row and who knew I could be so lucky? Brad was at the bus stop without Elise, again. Even better, the other two weren't. The gods were truly smiling on me. But I knew I needed to chill out. *Down, girl*, I told myself.

Seeing Brad made me glad I'd bought some Exlax yesterday and crapped out at least a pound or two. I had to be looking thinner, even though the scale wasn't changing much. Even so, Brad had said I looked good yesterday. Probably he was just being nice. Anyway, I knew Elise would be a tougher critic. Women always were.

Brad started walking over to my car. I got out hastily. I didn't need him to see the mess inside: the old coffee cups, crayons, DVDs, along with remnants of old Happy Meals. I knew Elise's car never looked like this. Note to self: clean car, ASAP.

"Hey, Brad," I said, striding over to him in order to put as much distance as possible between the car and us.

"Gail. You're early."

Why did he sound surprised? What the hell? Did Elise tell him I was always late? "Yeah. Surprise, surprise." I tried to keep my voice light.

His eyes swept over me and I could tell he liked what he saw. "You are a surprise. I mean, don't take this the wrong way, but you're kind of like the girl next door—but then you look closer and it's like, yeah, if we lived next to Hugh Hefner."

My eyebrows went high with surprise. Was he saying I looked like a Playboy Playmate? I mean, that was too much. Yeah, I did have nice breasts, but he couldn't actually be like referring to them, could he? My cheeks felt kind of hot.

Thank goodness, just then Ronnie walked out of her house and Kelly pulled up at about the same time. I had wanted to be alone with Brad but now I thought that might be a bad idea. A dangerous idea even. Still, a little thrill went through me as I remembered his comment.

Ronnie got to us first. She looked at me and I saw her take in my less-than-pale cheeks. The woman missed nothing. Why wasn't she a freaking detective or private investigator?

"Gail. You're early. Any particular reason?" She glanced briefly at Brad.

I made myself shrug. "No reason. Just ..."

"Brad! You're here again?" That was Kelly, who had quickly marched over from her car.

Ronnie and I shared a surprised glance because Kelly sounded so un-Kelly like. Like she was worked up over something.

Brad raised his eyebrows. "What's the matter, Kelly? Are guys not allowed here? Is it ladies' night or something? Are the Chippendale dancers arriving soon?" He had a teasing look in his eye that was so sexy. *Down, girl.*

Kelly looked slightly embarrassed, possibly by her odd tone earlier. "No. Definitely not." She paused. "Anyway, Beth brought her husband this morning." She glanced at Ronnie, as if wondering if she had just messed up. Oh, give me a break. Like we couldn't say what we wanted?

"Beth? Who's Beth?" Brad looked confused.

"Hello? The new mom?" Ronnie supplied. I admired her ability to be sarcastic with Brad. Clearly the woman had steel ovaries.

"Oh. Toenail painting lady." He looked at me and grinned.

"Only she wasn't." I tried to stifle a return grin.

"Nice guess though."

"Well," Ronnie said, "we can play the same game today because she just pulled up and she isn't getting out. Again."

We all snuck glances and saw Ronnie was right. Brad smiled but it was a slightly evil one, reminding me of his wife. Maybe some of her personality had rubbed off on him. I didn't like that possibility.

"I'm tired of that game," he said, "and anyway, she's obviously reading." Sure enough, we looked again and saw she had her head buried in a book. Brad muttered, "That's not allowed. Not on my watch." He strode toward to her car.

"What's he doing?" Kelly whispered, sounding panicked.

Ronnie shrugged, looking unconcerned. But something else. The corners of her mouth were turned up as if fighting a smile. What was up with that?

We all watched in fascination as Brad knocked on Beth's window. Then we all stifled giggles—or didn't stifle them actually—when she jumped in surprise.

She rolled down her window looking kind of annoyed. We inched closer to catch Brad's words.

"Hi. I'm Brad." He sounded like a guy on some dating show, and believe me, I wished I could be a contestant. I expected him to go on with, "I enjoy long walks on the beach and candlelight dinners."

Beth had an expression that looked confused and annoyed. "Um. I'm Beth."

"Nice to meet you, Beth." He paused then said, "Wanna come over and meet the gang?"

She made an expression that pretty much said she'd rather chew on barbed wire, but she got out of the car— pausing to check on her sleeping infant in the back—and then walked with Brad the few steps to our group. Brad started introducing everyone but we stopped him, explaining we'd been there, done that.

That surprised him. He turned to Beth. "Well, you must have heard about my end-of-summer party, then, right?" His party? The man was delusional. It was clearly Elise's party.

Beth only shook her head.

"Oh. Well. It's this Saturday at one. And if I do say so myself, it is the place to be. It'd be great to see you there." His eyes swept the length of her. "We have a pool. So bring your bikini."

Beth's cheeks turned pink. Yes, Brad definitely had that knack. He knew how to make the ladies blush. And no doubt other things. *Girl, get a grip.*

I'd been so busy watching Brad that I forgot about Ronnie and Kelly. I looked now and caught them exchanging a significant glance that meant ... who the hell knew what. But I guessed Kelly must be freaking out. I doubted Brad inviting Beth would be cool with Elise. It didn't seem Elise had told Brad anything about Beth, so he couldn't be acting on her orders. No, he was just being his flirty, spontaneous self. I didn't mind when it was directed at me. But with Beth? Oh, no. I mean, I was the only playmate of the bunch.

Er, that sounded wrong.

THE INFORMER

Wednesday morning I had the kids ready in record time. Working on a plan always made me more efficient in all areas of my life, especially since all the pieces were coming together. When I thought of how easy it had been, I was tempted to laugh like an evil scientist, but I restrained myself. That would have been too weird, even for me.

Brad inviting Beth was unexpected, but I soon realized he'd done me a favor. Although Elise would be upset that he'd made a move without her okay, she'd get over it. Especially when she saw what I had planned. But I needed to move quickly. I knew I could make it happen, but I needed still more pieces to fall into place. Most of them I could control, but some would be up to chance. I'd have to hope for the best.

I got outside and saw I was first. I heard a car, looked up, and saw it was Beth. Check. Another piece falling right in. This time I couldn't help it—I did laugh. Jessie glanced up from her book. "Mommy?"

"Er, yes, hon?"

"Was that your mad scientist laugh?"

I forgot that she and I joked about that sometimes when she read one of her books about, no surprise, an evil scientist. "Why did you do that? I'm not reading that book now."

Busted by my first grader. "Um, I'll explain later. Look, here's the new girl. Why don't you play?"

She rolled her eyes. "Brianna will be mad."

"Who gives a ..." I stopped myself in time. "I mean, I think it would be okay with her." It irked me to have to put it like that. Oh, how it irked me.

She looked doubtful.

"Look, you can blame me. Say I made you do it."

She was silent.

"Okay?"

"Okay," she whined.

Beth and her daughter walked over. The two girls eyed each other briefly, like wrestlers taking stock of their opponent. I gave my daughter a look. She sighed. To the little girl she said, "Come on. Let's play," sounding more bored than anything else. But they ran off together.

There was an awkward silence.

I smiled. "Well. So, how do you like the neighborhood?"

She looked like I'd just asked an extremely loaded question. Which I had.

"Well, it's ... interesting."

That was an intriguing choice of words. I waited but she said nothing else. I leaned in toward her as if about to share a secret. "You know, I can guess what you're thinking."

"I doubt it."

I gave her an appraising glance. It wasn't the response

or the tone I'd expected. "Look, I know we haven't been all that nice. But you should know that we're not all like that."

"Oh." She looked like she wasn't sure what to say.

"We don't all think like Elise or necessarily agree with everything she does. I just wanted you to know that." I smiled my most sincere smile, surprised I remembered how. Vaguely, though, I wondered: Is it still sincere if you're faking it?

Finally, she smiled back. "I'm ... glad to hear that."

"And some of us are worth getting to know if you give us a chance." I paused as if considering whether to say more. "And there are ... benefits of being in our little group." I saw her eyebrows go up.

We turned as the other women arrived. This was the part I was unsure about. How would Elise be?

"Good morning." Elise issued the general greeting as she walked over with her compatriot. But she sounded neither warm nor fuzzy. I guessed Brad had told her what he did. Still, I knew she wouldn't un-invite Beth. That would be too uncool.

Gail walked up to complete our group. There was an awkward silence as we all took in the fact that Beth was part of our circle today for the first time.

Elise turned toward Beth and smiled—but it was neither warm nor friendly. It was really more like baring her teeth like a lioness. "So. I hear my husband—he's just the cutest thing—invited you to our little shindig."

Beth nodded, "Yes, but I ..." and she seemed about to supply an excuse, which was smart of her. But that couldn't happen; I needed her to be there.

"So. I hope you'll be able to join us, with the whole family of course. Since I've already bought more goody bags for the extra children. Along with more food. I believe you have an older son?"

"Yes, but ..."

"I hear teen boys eat like crazy."

"Yes, but ..." Was that all she could say? It was getting ridiculous.

"Well, I'm prepared, as always. Brad eats like a teenager, too. Then again, he works it off like one." She glanced at Gail, briefly. "If you get my drift. Anyway. It's all set."

I glanced at Beth and she looked like she was wondering how in the world she'd missed her chance to get out of the party. But I breathed a quiet sigh of relief.

Elise turned toward Kelly as if sharing something only with her but speaking loud enough for us all to hear. "Really, Brad is just too generous. One of his few failings. But at least I can count on him. So dependable. Unlike some others ..." She trailed off and sent me a look. "Well, not everyone can be like him."

Good thing, I thought. Then we'd all be obsessed with flirting and our sexual prowess.

But was she actually blaming me for not stopping Brad? Like I was supposed to control him? What about Yes-girl? Didn't Kelly live for stuff like that? Or Gail? No, she was too busy drooling over Brad. Give me a break. I had no trouble now turning toward Beth and rolling my eyes in plain sight of them all. I knew by the look on Elise's face that she'd seen it. But for once, I didn't give a damn.

CHAPTER FIVE

THE TARGET

I sat in my parked car outside the high school, waiting for Ricky. What was taking him so long? I would have called or texted him, but I'd stupidly left my phone at home. But, luckily, I'd left the two little ones at my mom's, since she could watch them for short stretches. So at least I didn't have to worry about them being bored waiting.

I stared at the building I'd entered almost every day for four years of my life. My time there felt like a lifetime ago, and yet in some ways, like yesterday. I knew there were people who loved high school, those for whom it was the best time of their lives. Rick seemed like that—loving high school, for the most part. But I hated it. Just looking at the large, institutional drab building brought back too many memories, most of them bad.

I turned on the radio, searching for a distraction. An old favorite song was playing, and I turned up the volume without thinking. But I soon found that the lyrics of the song only brought me straight back to that place and time I wanted so badly to forget. Suddenly I was feeling all the intense, angsty emotions of those years. The song brought it all back, in a way almost nothing else could have—that feeling of being small, scared, and unsure. The anger and fear of being a nobody.

These weren't exactly welcome feelings, yet I couldn't shut the song off. It had a strange hold on me; it seemed I needed to relive these long-forgotten emotions. But it wasn't only the release of pent-up feelings that held me captive, it was also that the song conveyed a certain defiance, which had been like fuel to my teenage self. Even now, I felt that defiance surging through me. Yes, in high school I'd been like a misfit, the lowest on the totem pole, but then, who's fault was that? Wasn't that a result of the worst tendencies of human beings, the song seemed to say. We—anyone who identified with the song—knew there was a better, kinder way to treat people. People should not be put in boxes or told who they are or where they fit in or, more importantly, where they don't.

Someone slammed a car door near me and I was pulled away from my thoughts. I looked at my watch, again wondering what was keeping Ricky. I couldn't wait much longer. I knew Mom got tired easily.

More minutes ticked by. I sighed. I really did not want to go in that hideous place. But feeling I had no choice, I gritted my teeth and got out.

I dragged my feet, literally. I just did not want to have to walk through those all-too-familiar doors. At least it was after school and most of the kids were gone. The school would have been harder to take with throngs of teens hanging around.

As I made my way to the entrance, with each step, with every crack I stepped over, memories flooded my brain. I could see the popular girls giggling and talking behind their hands, as they glanced at you and then went back to their gossiping. I saw the popular boys who didn't bother to notice you at all, which was both blessing and curse. Because you were exceedingly aware that at every moment you were being judged. And you always came up short. I saw the girls who had boyfriends, making out in the hallway, or just flirting, flaunting the fact that they had what you never would.

All too soon I reached the door, then hesitated. Finally, I squared my shoulders, pulled the handle, and went in.

Compared to the daylight outside, the darkness inside the building felt strange. While my eyes adjusted, I could smell the faint odors of dirty gym clothes, mildew, and pot. Nothing had changed. The place was still the same old hellhole. When my eyes were able to focus properly, the first thing I could make out, standing just a few feet away from me, was Brian Peters, a cool popular jock—one of the best-looking guys in high school, and he knew it. Exactly the kind of person I'd just been picturing in my mind's eye. Seeing him made all those feelings I'd been having rush toward me at a dizzying speed.

I decided to confront him before I lost my nerve. "Hey, Brian."

"Yes?"

"So, I guess you still think you're all high and mighty, don't you?"

"Excuse me?"

"I just wanted you to know that you—and your kind—treated me like shit. I mean, would it have killed you to just to say hi to me? Notice me in some small way and acknowledge my existence? Or, God forbid, even ask me out? But no. Because to you I was like dirt, right? No. I was less than dirt." I'd been struggling not to shout, to stay as calm as possible. Now, I let out the huge breath I'd been holding. Strangely, I felt better. It seemed getting all that out had actually helped.

"Um. I'm sorry. But I don't know what you're talking about, ma'am."

Ma'am? Why was he calling me that? We were the

same age. Back in Texas, "ma'am" was used a sign of respect toward women. But back east, "ma'am" was what younger people called older people. Was he saying I looked old? I looked closely at him. He was definitely the guy I remembered. The same uncannily blue eyes, the same light-brown hair. But he did look young ... really young actually ...

Oh. My. God. This wasn't Brian. Not the Brian I knew anyway. It must have been his ... son. How stupid of me. How incredibly stupid.

"Uh. I ... I'm sorry. I thought you were someone else ... um .... so sorry ..." I started backing up. My face felt hot, so hot in fact that I feared it might combust at any second. I backed away and turned, squelching the urge to run.

"Um, ma'am?"

I turned back at his voice.

"You wanna go get some coffee or something?"

Did I hear that right? Really? Now, when it's totally inappropriate, a popular jock asks me out. This is the kind of luck I always had when it came to the opposite sex. I managed to shake my head as I went outside and strode to the car. I climbed in and drove off before I remembered that I had never picked up my son. So, I drove back but parked in a secluded spot, only breathing a sigh of relief when I saw Brian Junior leave.

Two seconds later, Ricky came out. I thanked God he hadn't seen what just happened. We drove home and all the while I prayed this little episode wouldn't cause any problems. I wasn't even sure exactly what I'd said to Brian Junior, thinking the entire time it was Brain Senior. What stupid things had come out of my mouth? Had it sounded like I was asking him on date? I couldn't remember. I shuddered at the thought of what those women at the bus stop would say if they found out about this. I had enough problems without being known as the neighborhood cougar.

THE WANNABE

I got to the bus stop really early this time. But the third time was not the charm. I'd managed to beat everyone, lucky me, but when the first person showed up it wasn't Brad; it was New— er, Beth. Not exactly the person I had hoped to see. So, I lingered in my car even as she got out. With my luck she'd start talking to me and then I'd be accused of fraternizing with the enemy. Soon I saw Ronnie come out. Only then did I make my way over. But I wasn't exactly in a rush anymore.

As I walked up, they were already talking about something. Soon I realized it was Elise's party. More specifically, what to wear.

"So, if you're looking for a great suit, Marman's has it. A miracle but for less than half the price." Ronnie was apparently giving Beth fashion pointers. But directing her to a discount store? That was too weird. Ronnie was usually smarter about fashion than that. She wasn't in my league, but still.

"Oh. Well that does sound good. Almost too good." Beth was apparently impressed. Which meant nothing coming from her.

"It's the real deal, from what my friend told me. Makes a woman look ten pounds lighter." Ronnie paused then added hastily, "Not that you need that."

They were both ignoring me, which pissed me off. If someone was being ignored it should've been Beth, not me. I'd gotten way past that point.

Just then Ronnie turned toward me and said with a smile, "But some of us do." Her words were tricky. She could have simply meant herself. Or, could she mean me? Hard to tell, but I figured I'd give her the benefit of the doubt.

Beth was quick to say, "Oh, I need it alright. Unfortunately, I still have a little extra baby weight hanging around."

Maybe in some circles it was okay to say things like that. In this one, admitting your weaknesses would only come back to haunt you. But I was hardly going to tell her that.

"Well, this will take care of that. Guaranteed."

I couldn't stop myself from pointing out the obvious. "But Marman's? I mean, it's so ..."

Ronnie fixed me with a hard stare worthy of Elise's best. "Why pay more?" Then she laughed, realizing she'd just used the store's slogan. But I could tell her laugh barely touched the surface of her anger. Clearly, I'd pissed her off, but I didn't know why.

Because fashion was my passion, I was about to argue the point, when we noticed Elise and Kelly getting out of their cars. Elise looked shocked—momentarily anyway—to see us all present. Soon the look was gone but still I knew that being last wouldn't sit well with her.

"Well. Everyone's so earrrlllyy today." She dragged out the word "early" making it sound almost dirty, like we should all be ashamed. I thought her cheeks looked sort of pinkish, and I couldn't remember that ever happening.

Yes, someone was gonna pay for this. I just hoped it wouldn't be me.

I glanced at Ronnie, but she was calm and cool. "You decided not to send Brad today?" She paused a beat. "We've been enjoying his company lately." Here she glanced slightly in my direction. Shit. That didn't mean anything, did it? Or geez, was I becoming paranoid?

Elise raised her eyebrows. "Well, I didn't have any reason to today. The last two days I had hair and nail appointments ..." she trailed off clearly expecting to be properly complimented. I poured it on thick and loud, for once drowning out Kelly. I needed this more than she did.

I groveled until the bus came and hoped it was enough. I hoped I was forgiven. For what exactly, I wasn't even sure. But one thing was certain. I couldn't wait to get back home. Where the house rules were much more clear cut, especially since I'd made them. Elise's rules might be arbitrary, but they were set in steel. Break her rules, and there was hell to pay.

THE SIDEKICK

Elise seemed angry today, no doubt about being last to arrive. Ronnie should know better than always trying to outdo her. Even the newbie beat her today. That didn't go over well. Especially since she must still be peeved at Brad for inviting her to the party.

I still didn't get what was with him. Inviting Newbie Mom—I couldn't bring myself to think of her as anything else—to Elise's party. The man had nerve. Elise must have let him have it, and not in a good way, when she found out.

Not that we'd ever know. To the outside world, all would be smooth and perfect.

Ronnie seemed happy about it. She tried to hide it but I could tell. She wasn't as good as she thought she was. Her happiness was strange though. Clearly something was in the works. We'd just have to wait and see.

But Brad couldn't actually be in on it, could he? I didn't think the guy was smart enough for that. No, his invitation must've just played into Ronnie's hands. Somehow, someway.

But why did he invite her, if it wasn't part of the plan? It must just be his flirtatious ways asserting themselves, yet again. He would cause Elise trouble eventually. I couldn't help but wonder whether he already had. Had he cheated on her? There, the thought was out. But it still felt wrong of me to think like that. For Elise's sake I hoped he hadn't but I just had a hard time not wondering about it.

That had to wear on a person. I mean with Steve, I felt 99.9 percent sure he wouldn't ever cheat. That reduction from 100 percent was just the normal but very slight fear I'm sure most women carried. But with Brad, Elise's level of comfort had to be much lower. Had to. I'm not sure how low, or what Elise thought about these things because it wasn't like I could ever talk to her about it.

No, I definitely did not trust the guy. And Elise shouldn't either. But if I tried to warn her, would she thank me? I'd never find out what she'd do because it wasn't gonna happen. No one could tell Elise anything. You don't tell queens how to control their kings.

CHAPTER SIX

THE QUEEN BEE

I stood in front of the full-length mirror in my bedroom, checking for any signs of sagging. Or sogginess. Or cellulite. I breathed a sigh of relief. No to all three "s" words. It wasn't every woman my age who could still wear a bikini. Even Kelly, who had super abs—curse the woman—had a bit of cellulite in the thighs. But I hardly held that against her; it just made up for the killer abs.

Anyway, I was body-ready. I was ready in all other ways, too. A month earlier I had the menu planned and the party goods purchased but then Brad had thrown that curve ball. But after my initial anger, I calmed down. Somehow I guessed that Brad's surprise would turn out okay. Better than okay, if subtle hints from Ronnie were any indication. And judging from past experience, they usually were.

But even if Ronnie failed, I had my own methods. I didn't need her. It was just nice to have some intelligent backup. And they didn't come any smarter. True, warm and fuzzy was not her thing, but so what? She and I had that in common. It made for a perfect partnership. Well, not partnership, because that implied equality.

The doorbell rang, signaling the arrival of the first victim—I mean friend—which would be Kelly no doubt. The woman was always first. My loyal supporter. Dare I say too loyal? Not at all! Still. The woman could be over-the-top. But I'd take that over the reverse, any day.

"Hey, Kelly. Always the first to arrive. Can't stay away

from me, huh?" I heard Brad's flirtations from downstairs. But I didn't sweat that. If he was talking that loud, clearly there was nothing to fear. Besides Kelly could be trusted. More than the others.

I sauntered on down, putting extra swing in my hips. As expected, that drew Brad's eyes back where they belonged. I gave him a lingering kiss and then put on my cover-up in a show of modesty. I'd walk around in my bikini all day if I could.

Kelly air-kissed me while her daughter ran in. "Brianna," I called upstairs. "Our guests are here."

Brianna walked down the stairs, in a slow almost sultry way, even swinging her hips. Where did she get that trampy act from?

Oh. Right. But it didn't look like that when I did it.

Brad just chuckled at his daughter and then whistled in appreciation. Steve, Kelly's husband, who had followed his wife, coughed and looked uncomfortable. I went over to him and gave him a real kiss. Air-kissing was just for us girls. I caught Kelly frowning. Please. It was just a little kiss. Brad always kissed my friends, on the cheek. So, I was just returning the favor.

The bell rang, again. The rest of my posse arrived. Gail and Joe and Ronnie and Ian. With their little darlings in tow.

"Well. Everybody's here," I said brightly, after the mandatory kissing was over. I could tell no one wanted to contradict me, but clearly we were missing one family. I hadn't forgotten. I just liked to pretend I had.

Finally Brad spoke up. "What about the new lady? The toenail painting one." He grinned at Gail.

She grinned back, but at my frown, she stopped.

"Let's all go out back and get settled. She'll find us." I didn't want to admit I didn't get their inside joke. And I didn't want to wait anymore for Beth. She wasn't that important.

The food was already out and chairs by the pool with towels neatly placed. Everything was perfect, including the weather. Even Mother Nature couldn't defy me. As it turned out, everything went like clockwork that day. Looking back on it, I had no complaints. Oh, and Ronnie? I might just have to promote her. Clearly the woman was First Lieutenant material.

THE TARGET

Stupid party day was here. Need I say I did not want to go? True, the women at the bus stop had been suddenly nicer. For the last two days I'd been in their privileged circle. I'd been getting there earlier so I could talk to Ronnie, the only one in the bunch who seemed truly nice. And she had been helpful, even suggesting a bathing suit for the party from hell. It was like she knew I was freaking out over what to wear.

So I'd gone to Marman's and found the suit easily enough. And—thank you, Ronnie—the thing was perfect. Cheap, too. The suit was a miracle indeed; I did look thinner. Sure, I was no Elise or even the rest, but I'd felt a little better about having to wear a bathing suit. Not good, mind you. Just a little less suicidal.

Brad had actually said bikini. Get a grip, dude. I hadn't worn a bikini since back in the day and even then it was only with a lot of self-consciousness. I was never one of those women who could prance around wearing next to nothing.

Where the hell was Rick? I'd told him how badly I needed him at this event. He'd gone to Home Depot for lawn stuff. Trying to keep up with the Joneses in this neighborhood took lots of time and money. But he should have been back by now.

I got the kids together and left a note for Rick. With dragging feet, we left. I forced Ricky to go with me. I needed him for back-up, in case the women reverted back into witch mode. He grumbled under his breath, clearly not happy.

Selena was the only member of the family who fit that description. She skipped along, without a care in the world. I envied her. Meanwhile the baby kept letting out little wails as I pushed her in the stroller. Even she was fussy.

As we approached Elise's home, I noticed how it suited her perfectly. It was a large, newer colonial, like most others on the street. But hers had a noticeable distinction. It stood out from the others by its use of contrasting blocks of black and white. The competing colors resulted in a stunning, yet not very comfortable, effect. The house seemed formidable, rather like its owner.

I shrugged off those thoughts and forced myself to ring the bell. I felt relief when there was no answer. "Oh, well. No one's home ..."

Selena tugged at my arm. "Mommy, I hear them in back."

"Okay, hon. I'll follow you." Or not. Maybe I could slip out.

But Selena kept looking back to make sure we were

following her. We turned the corner and there they all were. It looked like a scene from *Better Homes and Gardens*, with cut-and-paste people put in. Everything was perfect. It was too good to be real.

Elise's sidekick happened to be the closest person to me. She looked away from me after our eyes met and I thought she was going to ignore me. But then she turned back. "Oh, hi, Brenda."

Brenda? "Um. It's Beth."

"Oh. Sorry." She laughed. "I'm terrible with names."

Out of the corner of my eye, I thought I saw Elise smirk. But when I glanced at her, whatever I'd seen was gone.

"It's okay. I'm terrible with them too." I paused, thinking it was safe to ask the next question. "What was your name again?"

She gave me a look that could have frozen water. "Kelly."

"Sorry ..." I started but she was already walking away.

Elise came over then and welcomed me and the kids. She was nice. Her voice was smooth and easy. I still didn't feel comfortable.

"Well, the kids are already swimming, as you can see." She looked at Selena. "So, go on and join the others." She looked at Ricky. "You must be hungry. Grab a plate." Then she winked at me like we were sharing some secret. Which was too weird. What, now we were friends all of a sudden?

Ricky wasn't likely to say no to food. He piled his plate high, his headphones never coming off his ears. So much for a backup.

Out of the corner of my eye, I saw an older girl with light-brown hair and cute features. I guessed she was middle school age. I also guessed she was Elise's older daughter. She was whispering with another girl. They seemed to be checking Ricky out. But he was engrossed in his food and his phone.

Elise led me to a table that was big enough for all the adults. Brad and all the women were seated there. The other husbands were mysteriously absent.

I soon found out why. "Brad, don't you want to play pool with the guys?" Kelly asked.

Brad shrugged. "I can play anytime. Why would I hang out with a bunch of guys when I can be surrounded by attractive women?" He laughed like it was the funniest thing.

Elise laughed along, even harder. "Yes, we spoil you, don't we?"

"Don't I know it, babe." He grinned at Elise.

"Well. Most of us anyway." What did that mean? I caught Kelly looking at me for a second. Was that some insult against me?

Just then Brad focused his gaze on me, and it reminded me of a killer dog zeroing in on his prey. "So, Beth. How's it going?"

The words might have been just a friendly question, but the look and the tone said otherwise. Plus, why was he singling me out? "It's going." I laughed weakly, and by myself.

"Where's your hubby?"

"He should be here. Soon." Please God, get here, Rick. "He just had some lawn stuff to buy."

Brad laughed shortly. "He should hire someone. Tell him to talk to me. I'll hook him up."

"Um. Thanks." Yeah, I was pretty sure Brad was good

at hooking up. All sorts of hooking up.

"Your kids are so tan." I looked toward the voice. It was Gail, looking at me with an unreadable expression.

"Yeah, they are." There was silence, like they were all waiting for more. "They tan well." What was with these people?

"Are they adopted?" That was Kelly. With an innocent, wide-eyed look.

"Um. No." What the hell?

I guess from my one word, or two if you count "um," they could tell I was annoyed.

"Sorry." Ronnie spoke up. "It's just that they don't really look like you."

Brad laughed. "Yeah. You've got the coloring of ... well, like Belle. You know, from *Beauty and the Beast*. But your kids are more like ..."

"Maybe Aladdin?" Gail supplied.

I laughed but it wasn't from humor. It was from not knowing what else to do. I guess that gave them permission to laugh "with me" because they all joined in.

Brad looked at me, more intently if that was possible. "You look kind of familiar, actually."

Shit. "I get that a lot." I really hoped it was just my often-noted general familiarity that caused Brad's comment. I did not want to be remembered.

Ronnie cleared her throat, drawing my attention briefly to her. She was staring at Kelly, and I could have sworn some kind of nonverbal communication was going on between them.

Kelly spoke up then. "Brad, you should know this."

Brad looked at Kelly. "What do you mean?"

"Here's a hint. Think football, cafeteria food, and

cheerleaders."

Ronnie smirked. "Not in that order, of course."

Brad's brows came together, looking at me. "You were a cheerleader?"

"As if," Gail spoke the words under her breath but still loud enough for me to hear.

Kelly rolled her eyes. "No. Quite the opposite actually."

Brad snapped his fingers, still looking at me. "We went to high school together?"

He didn't remember me. He'd just finally figured out Kelly's oh-so-difficult puzzle. But what did Kelly saying "quite the opposite" mean? How would she know what I'd been like in high school? She hadn't gone to my school. Brad was the only one here who had.

"Yes, we went to the same school." I didn't want to admit it, but I had no choice. I wondered how Kelly knew.

"Hmm." I could see Brad's wheels turning. "Wait, I remember now. Weren't you voted something? I forget what it was."

Shit, shit, shit. This was one of them—those ghosts I feared. "No, not me. I was nobody. But you were voted something impressive right?" I was deflecting, hoping being reminded of his superiority would save me.

Elise was grinning. "Yes, Brad was voted 'best body' and he would have gotten 'best looking' but they couldn't give two of the best awards to the same person."

Ronnie snorted. We all looked at her. "Elise, you realize those aren't actual awards."

"What do you mean?" Elise's perfect brows rose.

Ronnie's usual blank face showed some signs of impatience. "The actual awards are given out when they announce the scholarships and the award for the highest math grade and science ..."

"Oh, you're talking about the academic awards." By the emphasis she put on academic, you could tell what she thought of those. "I'm referring to the awards that people actually cared about. Anyway, Brad was the king of the popularity awards from what I hear."

Brad nodded. "Yeah, but I was robbed. They gave 'best looking' to Brian when it should have been mine."

Kelly looked at me. "Beth, you knew Brad back then. You think he should have gotten best looking?"

Why was she bringing me back into this? Caught off guard I stumbled, "Um ... sure ... yeah."

Brad snapped his fingers again, looking at me intently. "Now I remember what it was. You were voted 'class wallflower.'"

There it was. The ugly ghost had risen. I stared at my flip-flops, my face feeling hot. I'd always hated that designation my peers had given me. And now, it had to be shoved in my face again years later. Really?

All the women giggled at this new bit of trivia, either oblivious to my suffering or, more than likely, enjoying it. Elise asked, "Class wallflower? They give an award for that? That's ridiculous."

Ronnie smirked. "Yes, I'm pretty sure that's the intent."

Gail shook her head. "But the awards are supposed to be good things. Wallflower? What does that even mean?"

"Not called awards," Ronnie said under her breath.

Kelly was also smirking. "Pretty sure it means someone who doesn't get noticed, or who never has a date. Stuff like that."

Ronnie responded, "Thanks for the clarification, Kel."

Oddly enough, my misery from this sad fact from my past being resurrected was ended by Elise herself. "Well, Beth, you and I are pretty much just the opposite, which of course seemed rather obvious even before. But now we have some actual proof. I was too modest to mention this earlier, but I was voted one of the best awards: 'most popular.'"

"Oh, very impressive," Kelly chirped, and the rest immediately joined in with their congratulations for something that happened years ago. It seemed proof that, for better or worse, high school is never really over. But at least the attention had been drawn away from me and my sad "award."

With all this talk of those old high school days, my thoughts turned to Sara, no doubt because I could really use a friend. Like now. I blinked my eyes hard. I would not cry in front of these people.

Brad turned to me just then about to dish about the old days, I guess, but Elise suddenly stood up and took off her cover up slowly and seductively. "Let's swim."

As if on cue, all the women disrobed. Which was, in a word … awkward. Brad's eyes seemed to want to be everywhere at once.

I followed suit, pun intended, but I cringed inwardly. And avoided everyone's eyes. Especially Brad's.

We made our way into the water. The temperature was perfect. I ducked my whole self in to cool off, since it was a warm day. I glanced around, and everything—the pool and the landscaping all around us—was like something out of a celebrity's house. It took on a dreamlike quality. I almost forgot where I was and who I was with. Then IT happened. And suddenly the "dream" turned into a nightmare. Actually, worse, because I couldn't pinch myself to wake up from the horror.

I swam over to the shallow end and stood next to Ronnie, hoping to talk with the one person who'd been nice to me. I heard some snickers. I didn't know why or even that they were directed at me.

Until Elise spoke. "Why, Beth. It appears you've found something in my pool. Maybe a wonder bra?"

Kelly chimed in. "More like implants."

What did they mean? Everyone was staring at my chest, including Brad. I looked down and saw what had caught their eyes. My normally B sized breasts had somehow grown to rival anything Pamela Anderson had to offer. I was suddenly a D cup. I looked again. Maybe a double D. Is there an E?

Events after that were a blur. A horrific, confusing blur. Let's just say it was a party to remember for many. But for me, it was one to forget. As if that was possible.

THE INFORMER

The plan worked perfectly. All the pieces fell in place, so quickly and easily, it was mind-boggling. Looking back on it now, it seemed a masterpiece. If a day in the life could be a work of art, then surely this one would be hanging at the Met.

I sat down to a well-deserved cup of coffee and to contemplate the events of that afternoon. Beth had taken the bait. That part had been quite out of my control. Silly Gail had almost ruined it with her fashionista leanings. I learned about that particular bathing suit's um ...

enhancements from an acquaintance. She told me about how the padding in the chest held water kind of like a regular diaper would, hence causing it to expand. Greatly. I'd filed that info away, knowing it would come in handy some day. I just didn't know it would be so soon.

But I hadn't stopped there. I'd done a little digging into Beth's past. I'd figured out about Brad and Beth going to high school together. In the back of their yearbook I found what she'd been voted. I'd fed that bit of trivia to Kelly and reminded her to make use of it, not wanting to do all the dirty work myself.

I had spent some time studying the pictures in their yearbook. It was funny, Brad looked almost the same. Had the guy found the Fountain of Youth?

As for Beth, she'd changed. Not drastically. It wasn't like she'd gone from homely girl to glam girl. Even with her new fashions, she wasn't glam. And surprisingly the girl in the picture wasn't homely. There were changes that didn't have to do with age. It was that she seemed more comfortable with herself now. The girl in the picture seemed to be saying, "Please like me." The woman today wasn't exactly overflowing with confidence, yet it was like she was saying, "This is who I am." Suddenly a weird thought flitted through my brain: I hoped we wouldn't destroy that.

I shook my head. What was with me? Was I suddenly developing a conscience? That would not do in my business. Besides, I wasn't the queen. This was all Elise's doing. The blood was on her hands, not mine. I mean sure, I played a part—a huge one actually—but it was all for her. If she wasn't here, none of this would be happening. I found myself pondering that—a world without Elise. There would be definite advantages in a world like that.

Ian walked in. "Some party, huh?"

The man had a gift for understatement. But then, he didn't know the half of it. Even the quarter of it. I shrugged. "Yeah."

"I felt sorry for that woman, though."

I didn't know he knew about that. I thought he'd been safe in Brad's game room, away from the battleground. "Yes. It was unfortunate." I went for a casual tone. "But she'll get over it."

"I guess." He shook his head. "But the poor lady ... with her um ..." He trailed off as he made motions toward his chest. I squelched the urge to laugh at the picture he made. He shook his head. "And all of you girls watching. Brad, too."

Ian was so sweet. Too good, almost. *Maybe I don't deserve him.* Where did that thought come from? I was a good mom, a good wife. Yes, I sometimes did things that weren't that nice, but then, I had no choice. Not if I wanted to help my daughter to have what I didn't.

Anyway, I was going to fix this. "Ian, look. I plan to befriend the woman. And with my help, she'll get over it. I'll see to that."

Ian looked like he didn't understand, which he didn't. But what I said was true. She'd be my friend again. I'd gain her trust, that much I knew. I didn't know how long it would take, but she would be eating out of my hand again. Elise could never accomplish that. People never trusted her after she burned them. But I was different. Better.

Anyway, I sort of viewed it like cleaning up Japan after we dropped the bomb. I'd help her get back on her feet. It was the least I could do.

CHAPTER SEVEN

THE WANNABE

Monday morning came, bright and early. Well, not bright. It was dark out and pouring. We needed the rain. I needed it too.

Not that I was a plant or something. It's just that sometimes I welcomed rain. It gave me an excuse to stay in my car. I could say I just didn't feel like getting out and standing in the downpour and ruining my clothes. Elise would accept that excuse, even though she always stood there with her umbrella. In her designer raincoat and her high heeled boots. With her BFF by her side, dressed just like her.

But I could huddle in my cozy car. I could even be late, well, later, anyway, and I'd hear none of her taunts. I could let Nina wear what she wanted, again using the rain as an excuse. Why ruin good clothes on a shitty day like this?

It was odd to feel like this. These were my friends, weren't they? I should want to go out there and catch up. Stand around and shoot the breeze with the girls. But it must be the rain. It puts everyone in a foul mood. Or, at least, an uncommunicative one.

I thought of Elise's party. I had laughed with the rest of them at Beth's discomfort. Joined in with their taunts during and after she left. But to be honest, my heart wasn't in it. I mean her chest blowing up like that *was* funny. But we didn't need to rub it in. We didn't need to be so ... heartless. The woman had feelings. I remembered all too well my own time in the trenches. What they'd done to me.

And was it worth it? It was a question I asked myself nearly every day. On days like this, I wasn't sure what the right answer was.

I wish I had more nerve. Sometimes, I wish I had the guts to stand up to Elise. To tell her what I think—to defy her even. But then, I'd be back at square one. I'd lose my privileged status. Worse, so would Nina. And Elise would find someone else. Another mother and daughter. We were just so replaceable. Maybe that's what bothered me the most.

THE QUEEN BEE

"What was with Gail?" I showed my annoyance, despite myself. I liked to play it cooler, usually.

Kelly raised her eyebrows. "What do you mean?"

"Hello? Staying in her car like that?" Where was Kelly's brain?

Ronnie snorted. "You know Gail. She doesn't want to ruin her designer duds."

"Please. A little rain won't hurt." Now Kelly snorted. "What is she, the wicked witch? Like she'll melt?" She was clearly working to undo any ill will from asking the clueless question before.

I smiled at her, letting her know all was forgiven.

Ronnie said slowly, "No. *She's* not the wicked witch."

I snapped my head toward her. Was she actually implying what I thought she was?

Ronnie laughed, in a careless way. "'Cause I've already taken that title."

Although she looked innocent enough, I wasn't sure I

believed that's what she meant.

Ronnie kept her eyes fixed on mine, her smile firmly in place. "But I'm surprised at Gail. You'd think she'd want to gloat about our success with the rest of us."

"Yes. Well. Her loss." I was peeved at Gail, more than Ronnie at the moment. I liked to have all the girls present during a gloating session.

Kelly officially began the gloating. "That party was something. I mean ... we really put it to her."

I felt Ronnie deserved some thanks, despite her questionable "wicked witch" comment. "It was rather amazing." I nodded toward Ronnie, telling her with my eyes that she'd outdone herself.

Ronnie nodded in reply, saying nothing. But I could tell she wasn't immune to my compliments, both verbal and nonverbal.

"I guess that's why she's missing in action today." Kelly said, stating the obvious.

"Yes, poor thing. She needed a day off, no doubt. After all the ... excitement from the weekend."

Ronnie was quiet, but I sensed her mind was busy in thought.

Kelly asked the question on all of our minds. "Do you think she'll stop? Coming here, I mean?"

I frowned. "No. I don't think it'll come to that." It was delicate business. There was a line of just how far you could go without crossing over. Everyone had their own line, their own level of tolerance. I didn't know where Beth's line fell. Determining people's tolerance level was part of the game, an art almost. But I trusted Ronnie. She knew how to flirt with the line but not cross it. After all, she'd learned from the best. I sent Ronnie a look.

Ronnie nodded again. "She'll be back." Now she sent me a look. And I knew we understood each other. One way or another, Beth would be back. Ronnie would make sure of that. Because we weren't done with her. Not by a long shot.

THE TARGET

I lay awake in bed. I'd skipped the bus stop today and driven Selena. I wasn't making a final decision. Then. But now I knew. I was done. To hell with those bitches. That might be harsh but then they deserved that name. And just about any other nasty name my brain couldn't help dragging up out of the gutter.

What really burned me about the whole thing was Ronnie's part. She had obviously set me up. Yet she'd seemed so nice. How could I have been so wrong about her? How could I not see what she really was? Because the person I thought was an angel turned out to be a much different kind: the angel of death.

Maybe we could sell our house and move to another part of town. Everyone here couldn't be like this. There must be some decent people in this town. Somewhere. Maybe they were hiding from the women in my neighborhood.

My mind went back to the party for what felt like the millionth time. How I felt when I left. How I'd dropped the kids at home, letting Ricky babysit for once. And how I'd driven around trying to make my car into a sanctuary. But no sanctuary could make up for that horrible afternoon.

At least Rick had never shown. At first, I'd been mad

about that. Then just really grateful. And not only because he missed watching me give new meaning to the term wonder bra.

My brain began replaying the details of that horrific day. Details I wanted desperately to forget. But when I tried to hit fast forward, it was no use. My brain was obviously into self-punishment.

I could feel the stares of everyone and the heat burning my cheeks. I had only one coherent thought: escape—as quickly and painlessly as possible. Well, painless was impossible, but quick was still doable. I hurried out of the pool, trying to block the noise from reaching my ears, but I couldn't help but register it. Their laughter. Their obvious enjoyment of my total embarrassment. Their stupid jokes. Like ...

Tormentor #1 – "Do you have any water balloons?"

Tormentor #2 – "We've got two. Beth's boobs."

I threw my bag over my shoulder and started running. But then I noticed my newly minted jugs shaking in an unnaturally scary fashion. I slowed to a quick walk, opened the house door, and stepped inside, breathing a sigh of relief to be out of their sight.

Only then did I remember my children. I groaned in frustration, realizing I had to go back. I put a hand on the door but decided to at least cover up first.

But I'd left my towel on the chair. That was the first problem. The next was that my shirt wouldn't fit over my new accessories. I could hear the fabric giving way when I tried to pull it over the huge things. I swore in frustration and took off searching for a bathroom to get the offending suit off me.

I found one, off of a large fancy bedroom. It clearly

wasn't the main bathroom, but I didn't have time to find the one for guests. I quickly changed into my clothes, opened the door, and walked right into something. Actually, someone.

Brad smiled. "What's your rush?"

"Brad." My stomach sank as I realized whose bathroom I'd used. "Um. Sorry. I didn't know where the main bathroom ..."

He waved me off. "Don't worry about it." His feet were firmly planted. I tried to step around him, but he moved the same way I did.

I tried the other way. He did too. This went on a few times. "Um. Brad, what are you doing?" I didn't get what he was up to although my stomach was still feeling funky.

"Dancing with you?" He grinned. But when I didn't grin back he looked more serious. "I just ... wanted to check on you. Make sure you were okay."

I almost rolled my eyes. Like he cared. But when I met his eyes I saw something there that surprised me. Something almost like kindness. Maybe because I'd seen so little of that today, I almost believed him. "Um, okay. You checked. I'm ... fine." That last part was a total lie, but I hoped it would get him to leave.

It didn't. He gave me a once-over. "I noticed."

"Where's Elise?" I thought a mention of his wife might pull him out of his—what I finally realized was a—flirtation.

He just shrugged. "She's busy with the others. Laughing and shit." He went on quickly, "But honestly? I thought you looked hot. Before and after."

I couldn't believe he was saying this stuff. My shock made me momentarily silent.

"You know, I do remember you."

"What do you mean?" I knew I should push past him but for some reason my feet stayed where they were.

"From high school. You were cute then. But you're even cuter now."

He stared into my eyes and suddenly it was like my brain went into some kind of deep freeze where no logical thought could penetrate.

Because it was like I was thrown back in time. And now, the best-looking guy in high school was paying attention. To me. Staring at me like he thought I was hot. Actually telling me I was hot. Then he was putting his hands on my waist. Leaning toward me. Then, his lips were on mine. His right hand moved up. I felt it cup my left breast. Finally, just as his thumb circled my nipple, my brain broke out of its freeze.

I forced myself away and shoved him hard. I heard footsteps then, the pitter-patter sound of bare feet moving away from us. I used Brad's momentary confusion to grab my bag and run past him.

I glanced over my shoulder but he wasn't following. I ran to the pool, quickly collected the kids and left.

Now, along with the sick feeling in my stomach because of what I'd done, I remembered those footsteps. And the thought instilled fear into my heart and soul.

THE SIDEKICK

I hadn't lied to Elise. That party was something. But not for the reasons Elise thought I meant. Yes, Beth had been humiliated. It was a triumph of the first order for Elise and

Ronnie too. Clearly Ronnie had her hands in it. Big time. Up to her elbows in the stuff. For some reason Elise didn't want me to guess how much. She avoided thanking her outright, but I could tell. Did she think I don't have eyes?

Maybe Elise almost deserves what happened at the party, later. I mean does she really treat me like an equal? I am her biggest fan, her most loyal supporter. I would never make a "wicked" comment like Ronnie did. Yet, does she appreciate me? Or does she just take me for granted? I didn't want to dwell on the answers to those questions.

But I couldn't help it. Just thinking rebellious thoughts about her made me feel guilty. No, it was too ingrained in me. I was who I was. Elise's BFF—if thirty-somethings can use that middle school term. And like it or not, it was what I'd be till the end. For better or worse.

That is, assuming she never finds out about what I did at the party. But that's my little secret.

CHAPTER EIGHT

THE INFORMER

My plan to get back into Beth's good graces wasn't too sophisticated, I admit. In fact, phase one was very simple. It involved groveling—lots of it. But first I had to find her. I didn't want to just ring her doorbell. Most likely she wouldn't open the door anyway after seeing my face through the window.

It wasn't too hard to "run into" her. Her kids still had to go to school. But I gave her a week. To let her calm down and to let the memory fade a bit. On the following Monday afternoon I spotted her in the parking lot.

I followed her discretely and then walked up to her where the parents waited in the cafeteria for the kids.

"Hi, Beth."

She turned and I observed many emotions in a split second. Most were washed away quickly, but one remained: coldness. She nodded at me, seeming incapable of anything else.

I sighed. "Look, can we talk?"

Her eyebrows came together. "I don't really see the point."

"I want to explain." I caught her disbelieving look but hurried on. "I know how it looks. But I didn't know about that suit. Honestly." I used my most sincere, honest voice with a face to match. I'd practiced at home just to make sure.

"Sure you didn't. You have some land to sell me too? Swamp land, of course."

I laughed at her humor. The corners of her mouth seemed to want to turn up. That was an encouraging sign. "Beth, I'm telling you the truth." I'd always been a good liar. I could easily avoid all the telltale signs of the normal lying person. The darting eyes, the fidgety hands. I did none of that. I was smooth.

I went on, "A friend told me about the suit. How great it made her look and how cheap it was. But she never said anything about it um ... well ... you know."

"Yeah. I do know. Unfortunately. And now your whole gang knows too."

I shook my head. "They're not my gang."

"Right. What would you call them then?"

I had to give her something. "In a word ... necessary."

She cocked her head like I'd intrigued her. Clearly it wasn't an answer she'd expected.

I answered her unspoken question. "I admit it, okay. I'm using them. For what they can do for me. Even more, what they can do for Jesse. You can do the same, if you come back."

She shook her head. "Uh, thanks. But I'm not into self-punishment."

"Look ..." I started, but just then her daughter ran over to her with a big hug. Beth's face changed immediately into one of warmth and love.

My daughter was soon with me, doing the same. I wondered vaguely if I looked like Beth, if I had the same mom look. But then, I caught the look on her little girl's face when she saw my daughter. Suddenly the way back was so clear.

I addressed her daughter. "Selena, would you like to come over and play with Jessie today?"

Her face lit up, while the mother's darkened. In the meantime, I sent Jessie a look that told her she'd better go along with me. Or else.

"Yes! Mommy, can I?" Beth's little girl was giddy.

Beth looked uncomfortable. "Honey. I don't know. We were going to go ..."

"Please, Mommy!"

Beth sighed, watching her daughter's face carefully. Clearly she couldn't resist that look of sheer eagerness. Her next words proved it. "All right." She sighed. "Just for today." Her look toward me was complicated though. But I was good at deciphering such looks. My best guess for hers was, "Okay, I'll let her play. But don't think this means we're friends. And more importantly, don't mess with her. Or there will be hell to pay."

I would have answered to the last part, "Don't worry. I have some morals left. I know to leave children alone. I'm not a total monster."

THE TARGET

I couldn't believe I let Selena go with that woman. What was I thinking? But it was just so painful to see that look in Selena's eyes, her almost desperate look. She wanted so much to have a friend. I feared it was like looking into a mirror image of my own soul. Despite how much I wanted to believe I had matured and gotten past my lack of confidence in my youth, I knew that part of me still existed. I just couldn't seem to get rid of it. The "wallflower" in me was still there, still a part of who I was.

Ronnie actually seemed to be telling the truth, too. She

seemed genuinely sorry about the whole thing. I detected no dishonestly on her face or with her body language. Maybe she was telling the truth. If so, then I guess I shouldn't be so mad at her. Maybe I should cut her some slack. But, I'd keep my eyes open in the future. What's that expression? Fool me once, shame on you. Fool me twice, shame on me. I definitely didn't want to play the fool again.

The others still bothered me. Even if Ronnie was in the clear, a point I was hardly sure about, they weren't a group I wanted to be a part of. Not after everything that had happened. I mean what could they do for me? What was worth being treated so badly? I couldn't really think of anything that would make me want to try again.

I had avoided sororities in college at least in part because of the crazy initiations I'd heard about. But that at least made some kind of sense. It was tradition. And once you were in, the meanness stopped and you were an accepted part of the group.

Would this work the same way? Would the bad stuff be over after the initiation? Who knew? But it wasn't worth trying it, in my opinion. I wasn't in college anymore. I didn't need some group of women to help me navigate through life. Did I? Well, definitely not this group, anyway. No. It was safer to be on my own. Much safer, actually.

THE WANNABE

I pulled my jacket closer together, trying to block out the wind as I made my way over to the bus stop. It was cold today but clear. And cold was not an acceptable excuse to stay in the car. Not that I needed an excuse today. That strangeness from the other day was gone.

"How's it going?" I asked Ronnie, the only person who had arrived so far.

"Hi, Gail. You're early today."

If Elise or Kelly had said that it would have felt like a dig at my tardiness, but with Ronnie it didn't seem like one. At any rate, she was right. Now that Beth had been gone for a week plus, I had reclaimed my old "always last" place. It wasn't how I wanted to be known. So I decided to make an extra effort not to be.

And after that day last Monday when I'd hid in the car, I realized I was being stupid. These women were my friends. I'd been through the tough part, so I shouldn't be worried anymore. Or scared. And Ronnie, when alone, was the easiest to talk to. I did get the feeling that her mild manners masked a more complicated personality, but she had qualities that made you like her. She was a good listener. She was patient. Yes, she could be sarcastic at times, but it was a dry sarcasm that was just her sense of humor. Really she was nice. At least nicer than the others.

And there were a couple things I wanted to ask her, two unrelated things. I started with the easier one. "Ronnie, I thought I saw Beth leaving your house yesterday about five?"

Ronnie shrugged. "Yeah, her daughter came over to play." She talked as if she was discussing the weather.

But this was so much bigger than weather. I felt my draw dropping. She actually invited the newbie's daughter to her home—I mean Beth wasn't even a member yet. I'd been in the group for months before any of them had invited my daughter somewhere.

Ronnie raised her brows a little. "What?"

I knew she knew why I was so surprised. I wasn't sure why she was pretending she didn't. "Well. It's just ..." I trailed off, unsure what to say.

"Are you worried the queen won't approve?" She smirked, but it was clear she was smirking at Elise. "It's okay. I have it on good authority."

Now I shrugged. "I'm just surprised, you know?" Another reason I liked talking to Ronnie alone. She was the only one in our group who would sometimes put Elise down. Or at least refer to her with sarcasm.

"Well. Not to worry. All part of the 'master plan.'" She put master plan in air quotes making fun of her own words. She didn't take herself too seriously. I liked that about her too.

I decided I would ask the other thing. Knowing me, I might not have another opportunity to talk with Ronnie alone. I had a female question to ask, woman to woman. I had no sisters and my mom was out of the question because she'd blab to all her friends. As for close friends not in this group, I really didn't have any. I'd burned most of my bridges to be here. And I definitely wasn't going to ask Elise or Kelly. Ronnie was it, my only real choice.

"I was just wondering about something. Are your hormones going crazy?"

Another person would have looked at me like I had just sprung three heads, since I'd *really* changed the subject and also managed to make it sound like I was accusing Ronnie of being a cougar or something. She just raised her brows again slightly, looking more bored than anything else. Nothing fazed her.

But I wanted to clarify. "I mean, lately I just feel like

I'm so ... um ... well, like, I kind of want every guy." I laughed at myself. "I was wondering if that was normal. You know like part of growing older is having crazy hormones."

Ronnie smiled slightly. "You want *every* guy?" Just then she glanced toward the garbage truck up the street. Tuesday was garbage day. And garbage day meant seeing Warren Talbert's butt as he bent over to retrieve everyone's recycling bins. It wasn't a pleasant sight.

I laughed. "Okay. Not every guy." I paused. "Just every somewhat decent-looking guy."

But as my luck would have it, right then we heard a car pull up. It was Brad. It had to be Brad. Today. After I'd asked the raging hormone question. But even worse, Steve, Kelly's husband, was parking his car in Kelly's usual spot. That was both weird and really unfortunate given our current conversation.

I had a sinking feeling that I'd picked the exact wrong time to talk about this. I prayed I hadn't picked the wrong person, too. I exchanged a look with Ronnie. She said with a perfectly straight face, "Looks like today's your lucky day."

I chewed on my nail. "Look. Just because I said that doesn't mean ..."

But Ronnie started talking about the weather. Which was probably smart. I didn't want those two guys hearing what we'd just been talking about. So we suffered through a long weather conversation, as the guys struggled to get their charges out of the car and over to the bus stop. Women were so much better at that kind of stuff.

"Hey, ladies." That was Brad, giving us a both a sort of abbreviated once-over. Steve was by his side, like a male version of his wife.

Ronnie said, "Hi, guys."

I said, "Good morning," which I hoped was more disinterested sounding.

I couldn't wait for the sound of the bus. Usually having Brad there would be a good thing. Brad with Steve? Even better. But not now. Not after I'd opened my big freaking mouth.

But I had to admit to myself they both looked good. Two very attractive men—Steve was a policeman and was wearing his uniform. I had always been weak in the knees for a guy in uniform, even before the hormone problem. Then there was Brad, who required no uniform to look good.

We hadn't seen Brad since the party. "So. Some party, huh?" If I could get them all thinking about Beth, including Ronnie, so much the better.

Brad laughed. "Yeah. It was fun. Especially later." He winked at me slyly. What the hell did that mean? Nothing had happened that day, nothing between me and him. He seemed to be implying something had but nothing ... well, there was one little thing. But I'd been kind of drunk so it was hard to remember. I mean, not so drunk that I blacked out or anything. I remembered enough to know it was no big deal.

I looked nervously at Ronnie and saw a look I couldn't decipher, but then it was gone and she just looked bored.

I wanted to get Brad's mind on safer ground. "What'd you think of the exploding bathing suit?" I never thought I'd have to ask that outright. I thought Brad would have jumped at the topic.

Brad shared a look with Steve. "Yeah, Steve. You

missed that. It was really something. From B to Double D in seconds flat."

Steve laughed shortly. "Yeah, I heard about it." But something in his voice made me think he was bored with the whole thing. Like, yeah, it was funny, but it's time to move on.

Brad said, "But some women don't need those gimmicks. Since they've got the real deal."

I thought he looked at me out of the corner of his eye. But clearly he was referring to his wife. He must have been. Or not?

Anyway, my mission was accomplished. I had them off and running, all three of them discussing the finer points of Beth's misfortune, although it was mostly Brad and Ronnie doing the talking. I stayed quiet. And tried to contemplate the beauty of the early fall day. To watch the pure joy on the kids' faces as they chased after each other in a game of tag. Anything to try to subdue my raging hormones, which were showing absolutely no signs of slowing down.

THE QUEEN BEE

Wednesday morning the girls fawned all over my hair and nails, just like I'd expected. You'd think I'd get used to that, even bored by all the fuss and attention. But for some reason I never did. I enjoyed it just as much as ever.

Like usual, I tried to decide who laid it on thicker, Ronnie or Gail. I wasn't counting Kelly, at first. Usually whoever feels the guiltiest is the one who puts the pedal to the medal. But it was running neck and neck today. Then

Kelly joined in too, which made no sense since she had been there with me at the salon and had already done her fawning.

In the end, I couldn't choose the winner. So, were they all feeling guilty then? That was something I'd have to think about later.

After the compliment fest was over, Gail began a topic I'm sure she felt was similar to compliments in that I never tired of it either.

"So, Elise. I still can't believe that party. It was so amazing."

"Yes, it was quite the event." I had to appear like I agreed. Like I wanted to talk about it. But the truth was I didn't. After I'd been through Beth's embarrassment in my mind like a hundred times, I'd remembered some other things about that day. Some things that bothered me. Things I'd rather forget.

The discussion ran on though, with me keeping up the pretense. Finally it was over and we went back to our cars. But at home with nothing to do, my mind went straight to those troublesome thoughts.

After Beth left on party day, we drank some wine, just a couple glasses. Actually I'm not sure how many. I'm not normally a big drinker. For obvious body-related reasons, I just don't want the empty calories.

But a celebration seemed in order. So I drank—a little. Or a lot. It's hard to keep track, when your glass keeps getting filled before it's even empty. I don't think it was any more than three glasses. Maybe four.

Events became a little blurry after that. I don't like blurry; I like control. I like to be in the driver's seat always. But when the world becomes fuzzy, control is harder to achieve, if not impossible.

Here's what I do remember. Laughing about Beth with just the girls and then with their husbands, some of them anyway; I think some were still in the game room. Then yelling at Brad to go out and watch the kids who were in the pool for a while unsupervised. Thank God nothing bad happened. My reputation as a perfect parent was on the line.

Then I remember overhearing Jordan talking about Beth's son with her friends. Something about how hot he was. But I stopped that talk really fast. Need I say that no child of mine was getting involved with a Hispanic boy? Now Asian—I'd consider that. But definitely not Black or Hispanic. Just too ... something. I'm not a racist or anything. I just have high standards.

Then I remember going back inside, maybe for more wine, maybe to visit the little girl's room, I don't really remember. But I was passing by my bedroom and I heard voices. A lower male voice and a higher pitched female one. I hesitated outside the door for a minute or so. I wasn't really sure how long I stood there. Time was moving differently.

The hesitation was unlike me. I strained my ears trying to place the voices. The male one was all too easy—I knew my husband's voice. But the female one eluded me.

I took a deep breath and put my hand on the doorknob. Slowly I turned it. Locked. Something like relief washed over me. I felt like walking away. But my feet had other ideas and remained bolted in place. I knocked. Quietly at first but then louder when there was no answer.

After a minute or so—again not sure of the exact amount of time that passed—Brad opened the door, looking his same old laid-back self. "Hey, babe. Can't stay away from me, huh?" He looked normal. No flushed cheeks or messy hair. No undone belt. His shirt was untucked but then that's how he wore his T-shirts.

"Yes. I mean no. I ..." Good God, what was wrong with me? That's why I didn't usually drink. I sounded like Beth. I frowned, trying to concentrate. "Brad, I heard voices in there."

He laughed. "Yeah. That was me."

"Not voice. Voices. And one of them was female."

He laughed harder. "Female? Babe, I think you've had too much wine."

"Brad, I know what I heard." I was pretty sure I did anyway.

"Okay. You got me. I was singing. And some of the parts were falsetto." He grinned. "But don't worry, I won't start wearing your clothes."

The thing is, he was so convincing. He didn't look guilty at all. Before I hadn't been able to make out any of the words, so it was possible it had been singing I heard. It made sense, sort of. At least I thought so at the time, in my wine-induced haze. Anyway, there was no one in the room. I peeked in and it was empty. The bed was made; no person could have been hiding in the covers. There was only him, standing back with his arm extended as if inviting me in to inspect everything. But I didn't. That seemed too undignified. I was satisfied. Then.

But later I realized there were other possibilities. I hadn't checked our bathroom. Or under the bed. Or the closet. And because I'd believed him, I hadn't watched the door to see if anyone came out later. So I'd missed my chance.

It wasn't like me to miss chances, of any kind. It was either the wine or ... something else. I didn't want to think what that other something could be. So I decided it was definitely the wine. It had to be.

CHAPTER NINE

THE TARGET

"I better not regret this." I glared at Ronnie. I was back where I said I'd never go again. Ronnie had practically begged me to come back, saying she needed a friend with her in the trenches. A friend, she'd actually said. Maybe it was her use of that loaded word that convinced me more than anything else.

Well. There was another reason. But no way was I telling Ronnie about that. I wasn't that stupid. I had learned a few things.

"You won't. Trust me."

We were both here a little extra early because Ronnie had promised me a much-needed pep talk before the others arrived. As for trusting her, I guess you could say I was still working on that.

I sighed. "I still don't see why you put up with them."

Ronnie knelt down to tie her shoe. Jessie ran by, blowing a kiss at her mom and Ronnie gave her a rare, totally mom-like smile.

She stood back up. "Like I've told you before, being one of them opens doors."

I snorted. "You make it sound like going to Yale or Harvard."

"No, I'm not talking about career doors. I mean social doors. And they can be just as important—even more so."

"Not sure I follow you. I mean what can she really do for me?"

Ronnie gave me a penetrating look. "Look, were you

popular in high school?"

I smirked. "You're looking at the head cheerleader right here."

She smiled. "And I was voted most gullible." She smirked back. "Oh, and most likely to steal the head cheerleader's boyfriend."

I laughed. "That was you?"

"Seriously, I'll admit something to you. I wasn't popular. I was in a smart clique, not nerds ..." She trailed off with a look I'd never seen on her face, kind of sad, kind of angry. She appeared lost in thought for a moment or two.

The odd look left and she went on. "We were smart, but we certainly were not top of the heap. But my daughter? She'll be in the most popular group, because Elise's daughter will be. In fact, she'll own it. The seeds are already planted. And any children of Elise's friends will come along for the ride."

"But ... is it that important? Popularity? I mean at the time it seems like high school will never end, but it does. And then life goes on. Thank God." I said the last two words under my breath. But I knew Ronnie would hear me. Sometimes I swore the woman could read my thoughts.

"True enough. But wouldn't you like your daughter to have the high school experience you didn't? To be the type of girl that everyone looks up to and admires?"

"If they looked up to her for the right reasons, sure. But if it's just because they're afraid of her or because they like the way she looks or dresses, then no."

She nodded. "I give you a mental handshake for your answer, but still, I would ask, really?" She looked at me intently. "Did you go to your prom?"

I hesitated. I didn't want this to be true confessions from high school.

But my hesitation gave me away. "No, right? Well, wouldn't you want your daughter to go? And to not only go but to be one of the bells of the ball, like a true-life Cinderella?"

"I hate Cinderella," I blurted, thinking of Elise's resemblance to the famed princess.

Ronnie cocked her head, a slightly amused expression on her face. "Got Cinderella issues, huh? Okay, pick a different princess, then. Who do you like?"

I thought of Belle, but said instead, "Mulan."

"Why her?"

"She's tough. The girl goes to war, after all. You can't get much tougher than that."

"So you admire toughness. Then you should admire Elise."

"I admire toughness, not ..." I trailed off because I'd been about to say bitchiness. But I wasn't sure I wanted to say that about Elise in front of Ronnie. She was too close to her.

Ronnie laughed shortly. "I know, she's more than tough." She paused. "But it sucks to miss something like that, right? To have to sit home on prom night because you're not cool enough. No guy wants to ask you since they all want to go with the 'it' girls. Well, now our kids will be those girls. They won't be sitting home. Ever. Unless they want to." She paused again. "It's that simple."

I shook my head. I doubted it was that simple. I also doubted it was worth it even if she was right. Because the price Elise asked was too high. It was almost like selling your soul. Or like joining some radical group that demanded unconditional loyalty yet gave little in return.

We heard car doors signaling the arrival of the others. I braced myself for the polar opposite of a warm welcome.

Elise and friend strode over just as Gail ran over, checking her watch.

"Good morning, ladies," Elise issued a general greeting. I waited for something, an insult directed at my outfit, some comment about the group letting in "just about anyone" or something. But nothing came. Not even surprise that I was here again after my week plus absence.

Instead, after general greetings, Elise was off on some other topic.

"So, like last year, I'm again running for the president of the PTO. I don't expect any problems; after all, I was already president last year. However, just the same, I'd like you all to talk me up on social media. I'm sure you know what to say. But don't use Facebook only—use Instagram and Twitter too. And please be creative. I don't want everyone just repeating what everyone else has said." She paused. "That is, if you ladies wouldn't mind."

Kelly immediately chimed in. "Of course we will. The PTO is so lucky to have you."

Gail nodded, saying, "I would love to help you out," but I thought she looked a little unsure. Ronnie said a simple "Of course," keeping her poker face. I nodded, but said nothing. I didn't even have Instagram or Twitter, but I guessed Ricky could help me. I just wasn't that interested in social media stuff. It all seemed like a popularity contest, and I thought those ended with high school.

Elise nodded and smiled, looking pleased with our answers. "So, everyone needs to start working on it right away."

"Roger that." Ronnie seemed to be holding back a smirk.

I sent her an understanding glance. Because Elise's words were rather like orders.

Elise smiled, not seeing the withheld smirk. "I'll be checking to see everyone's progress in a few days." Here she glanced at each one of us in turn. Even me. Did that mean what I thought it did? Was I "in" now? A bonafide member of the inner circle? I guessed the answer was a qualified yes. But that realization did not instill any joy in my heart. In fact, it was just the opposite.

THE SIDEKICK

Well. I'm moving up in the world. Kicking ass and taking prisoners. Or ... something. I did something worthy of Ronnie herself. And why not? Like I can't? Like I don't have the brains she does? Or should I say, the balls?

Because of me, Beth is back at the bus stop. No doubt Ronnie will take the credit, but I know the truth. And Beth knows. And if I need to or want to, I can make sure Elise knows that she has me to thank. But for now, I'll stay quiet. Both about what I did and what Beth did. I'll bide my time and plan my next move.

Beth looked shocked. I enjoyed the look on her face. Even more, I enjoyed the feeling of having her under my control. In a small way, it must be how Elise feels every day of her life. I can see why she likes it. Yet, being the queen wouldn't do for me. I just want some respect, some acknowledgment that I'm just as important as Ronnie.

Actually, even more so. Because I am Elise's right hand, not Ronnie. Elise needs to remember that. If she doesn't, I might just have to remind her.

THE INFORMER

I picked up Jessie from Beth's house that afternoon. They'd begun having alternating play dates. For the first one, Jessie hadn't been thrilled. But now quickly—maybe too quickly—they were becoming friends. I had wanted—even needed them—to play together. But real actual friendship hadn't been my goal. I wasn't sure it was desirable or, for that matter, even achievable. Was real honest-to-goodness friendship possible? I doubted it. Therefore, I didn't want Jessie to think it was, only to be disappointed later when it inevitably failed.

But for now, anyway, I would let them play together. Gradually, I'd bring it to an end. Someday. I'd worry about that later.

Standing with Beth on her porch while waiting for Jessie, I asked Beth, "Well, is it so bad being back in the trenches?"

"I don't know. Not so bad I guess."

But her face seemed to say otherwise.

"Elise didn't say anything about you being back."

"I noticed. Isn't that odd?"

"Not really. For her, silence is about the best compliment you can get. It usually means acceptance. Of some sort."

She just nodded.

"But I thought I should warn you. About the next big

thing."

She raised her eyebrows and I saw actual fear in her eyes. "Is it horrible?"

"Depends how you look at it, I guess. It's a party."

"Then yes. That's pretty horrific." I could see that she was remembering the last one.

"It's a Halloween party this time. Elise and Brad are very into Halloween."

"How appropriate."

I couldn't help giving her a grin. "Yes, it is, isn't it? But just to fill you in on the details, every year Elise chooses a theme for the girls and then picks their costumes to go along with it."

"Are you serious? She tells them what they have to be?"

I rolled my eyes. "I know. It's a bit drill-sergeant-like."

"But the girls go along with it? Don't they want to have a say?"

"She picks stuff they like. It's not like she's telling them they have to be firemen or monsters. It's always girl friendly. Plus it's always something Brianna wants, and the girls are such little followers"—here I couldn't help but wrinkle my nose in distaste—"that they always go along with it."

I saw the look on Beth's face and, although she said nothing, I could guess what she was thinking. "I know ... if I want her to think for herself then why am I encouraging this whole arrangement?"

"I said nothing, Ronnie."

I snorted. "Your look said it for you."

"Well. Since you asked the question, I guess you should go ahead and answer it."

"Okay. Truthfully, I would like Jessie to think for herself. But she's young and has time to learn that. And for now, it's in her best interest to go along with the little ... diva."

Beth smirked at my use of that word. "Elise doesn't already have the theme picked, does she?"

"Are you kidding? She has it picked the day after Halloween. All ready for next year."

She looked apprehensive. "So, what is it?"

"It's all good. Princesses."

"Yes, Selena does like princesses." But suddenly she seemed to think of something. "You mentioned a party. For the kids only, I hope?"

I shook my head.

"But the grown-ups don't actually wear costumes, do they?" I could hear the fear in her voice.

I nodded. "Yup. They do." I paused. "That is, if they know what's good for them."

She rolled her eyes. "Does she pick our costumes, too?"

"No. That's up to you."

"So. I suppose you have some great costume to recommend for me. Like an exploding potato. Or a French Maid costume, complete with an always-occurring wardrobe malfunction."

I laughed, not worried because she didn't sound mad. "Brad would like that." I smirked. But I was surprised to see some color stain her cheeks. What did that mean?

"He'd like it better if someone else wore it. Like Gail maybe?" Her words were right, but I sensed she was working to cover up some emotion that had caused her flushed cheeks.

"I don't know about that. I've seen him giving you the

look."

"The look?" She eyed me warily.

"You know. The look he gives the female of the species when he's um ... in heat, shall we say. Which is always."

"What's the deal with him? I don't mean his flirting; I mean, why is he around so much? Doesn't he work?"

"Yeah, he works. You've seen their house. Clearly he's doing something right. Because she doesn't work."

"Yeah. But what's his job?"

"I don't know. A gigolo, maybe?"

That got a laugh out of her. But her cheeks still looked pink. I'd have to think about that later.

As far as her question, I knew what Brad did. But I wasn't sure I wanted Beth to know. I liked secrets. They often came in handy later. So I steered the conversation back to costumes. "So, anyway. You can wear whatever you want to Elise's Halloween ball."

I could tell from her face that fact didn't reassure her. And, well, it shouldn't have.

THE QUEEN BEE

Halloween was still a couple weeks away. However, preparation is the key to a successful party. Kelly volunteered to have the affair at her house. And I was okay with that. Especially since at her house I was still in charge. All decisions would be mine: the food, the decorations, and the all-important guest list. Although it would be the same as the summer fling, hopefully in more ways than one. But not quite in every way. Hopefully there'd be no weirdness with Brad. But then, I almost wondered if I imagined all that last time.

It was a princess theme, which Brianna picked and I wholeheartedly endorsed. I already knew which princess I'd choose. Clearly I had Cinderella written all over me. And Brad would have to be Prince Charming. Well, I put that kind of strangely. It's just that he had the wrong coloring. But, that one defect aside, he was my perfect prince, my knight in shining armor. Maybe we'd do a Camelot theme next year and he could actually wear a knight costume. That'd be pretty kinky in bed. But then it'd probably be hard to get it off him. And it would be uncomfortable. I mean, my naked flesh against that cold metal ...

Pulling my thoughts back, it was all about the kids. Halloween, I mean. Brianna had talked about being Jasmine, but I nixed that. Jasmine? I mean what was the girl thinking with her beautiful blonde hair? She was a born Cinderella. A chip off the old—I mean the new, gorgeous—block.

I pulled up to the bus stop, with Kelly right on my tail as always. Couldn't the woman give me just a little space? Did she think if she didn't keep close, she'd cease to exist or something? Maybe she would, actually. Her attachment to me bordered on ridiculous. I mean without me, would she even have a life?

Suddenly I realized these were strange thoughts to have about my best friend. That phrase echoed in my head. Best friend? Now there was a quaint term. Did such a thing exist? And was Kelly mine? Or wasn't she just like everyone else? Friends with me only because of what I could do for her? Even the modern phrase—BFF—was not so modern. What had they added to the original idea? Only an even more unattainable goal: friendship that lasts forever. Yeah, right. Good luck with that, girls. I thought of my old friends from high school. They'd scattered like snowflakes in a blizzard. Or maybe more like the way those wet snowflakes melt into nothing when they touch down on the earth.

I suddenly became aware that my "BFF" was standing awkwardly by my door, no doubt wondering what I was doing. I forced myself out of the car, and as we headed over to the group, I attempted to banish those momentary odd thoughts.

"So," I started after the typical greetings, "is everyone ready for the Halloween bash?" I glanced at everyone in turn but lingered on Beth. Normally I paid her little or even zero attention. But now, I hoped to catch something in her eyes. Surprise, or even better, fear. At the very least, some insecurity. After all, the last party hadn't exactly been a picnic for her. Well, it *had* been a picnic but, for her, a picnic from hell. Which was more appropriate for Halloween, actually. I suppressed a grin at my joke.

As Gail and Kelly talked up my party, I searched Beth's face. But I saw nothing. No surprise. No discernable fear or insecurity. It was an admirable poker face that could almost do Ronnie proud. That thought made me glance at Ronnie and I thought I saw the remnants of something eerily like support. Like Ronnie was giving Beth some kind of silent encouragement. But I had to be seeing things. Had to. Because Ronnie had better not be going down that road. Not if she knew what was good for her.

But clearly, someone had told Beth about the party. That much was obvious. Was Ronnie the tattletale? Or someone else? I'd have to think about that later. And when

I was sure who it was, I'd arrange the punishment.

THE TARGET

I got the kids off the bus and then went to visit my mom. She seemed in a good mood today. Somehow, despite her disease, she managed to be upbeat—most days anyway. Probably just for my benefit because that's what good moms do. They hide the bad stuff from their kids, even if those kids are adults themselves.

Anyway, my dad was home too, and so I left the three of them there so they could spend some time with their grandparents, but also so I could make a short trip to the local cheapo department store. Not Marman's. No way would I ever shop there again.

But I decided the other main cheapo store was safe. I pulled into the parking lot, relieved to have a little time for myself but also secure in the happy knowledge I'd be safe from seeing any of the bus stop women. They were definitely not cheapo department store girls.

I lingered in the baby section and picked up a few little things—socks, onesies, and the like. But then I remembered I needed underwear too. I was losing the baby weight, finally, but a lot of my underwear had been stretched out during that time, since I refused to wear maternity panties on principle.

So, I picked out some panties, nothing too Victoria's Secret, because that wasn't me, but not too old-lady-like either. I headed for the registers, but I stopped dead in my tracks upon realizing the only open register had a young male cashier. A young, attractive male cashier, at least from my quick glance. As I stood there doing a pretty good statue imitation, I told myself to think logically. Why would a young guy care that I was buying panties? It was just his job. He probably didn't even notice what middle-age women purchased.

So I squared my shoulders and headed over to the line. I positioned the baby stuff on top of the underwear as I held it and avoided looking at the cashier while waiting. Finally it was my turn. I put the items down on the counter, since there was no way I was handing my undies directly to him.

He said, "Hello," and I responded with something similar. Our eyes met briefly then. And my stomach dropped like I was riding the Drop Tower at the local amusement park. Because it was Junior. The boy I'd mistaken for his father that day at the high school when I'd been in the throes of some kind of horrible walk down memory lane. I looked away immediately and prayed he wouldn't remember me. But his next words confirmed the worst.

"Hey. It's you." He sounded surprised. And something else I didn't want to examine too closely.

He picked up the first baby item on my pile and started scanning. I wondered whether I could somehow swipe the undergarments from the bottom of the heap, without him seeing it. But that seemed difficult at best.

I didn't know what to say, so I just attempted a confused look. "What?"

He didn't seem to hear me. "You know, I totally don't get my dad."

I raised my eyebrows. What did that mean? No way was I asking him, though.

He answered my unasked question, anyway. "I would've asked you out. If you look like this now, you must have been smokin' back in the day."

My already warm cheeks felt like fire. I had no clue what to say. I was spared from coming up with something because suddenly a voice broke through my embarrassment.

"Beth? How are you?"

The too-smooth voice came from right behind me. I turned toward it, wondering how things could possibly get any worse. But I soon found out how.

Because it was Elise. Standing right behind me in line with a smile that could have been a smirk. No, that definitely was somehow both a smirk and a smile.

"Um. Elise. Oh. Hi." I couldn't even put together a "How are you?" I prayed that somehow she hadn't overheard Junior's comments.

"So." She glanced from me to Junior. "I take it you two … know each other?" Damn. Damnity, damn, damn, damn.

"No. Um. I mean, no. I don't. Know him, I mean." I sent Junior a silent plea. To keep his mouth shut.

It seemed Junior was on board. He nodded slightly at me, continuing to scan the items. He smoothly answered Elise at the same time. "I don't know her. We were just talking."

I wanted to get Elise talking about something else, to distract her from both Junior and the underpants on the bottom of my pile. "I didn't think you shopped here, Elise." I didn't care at the moment if I put her on the defensive— so much the better if it would help distract her.

"I don't. Normally. But I had some little items to

purchase. Like teacher's gifts, that kind of thing." She sounded smooth. Not at all defensive. Usually that would have been a good thing. But not now.

And she was so disgustingly prepared. It was early October but here she was buying holiday teacher gifts? I hoped she'd go on and brag about that a bit but she didn't. So it was quiet as Junior held up my underpants to begin scanning.

I tried to ask Elise more about those teacher gifts but she cut me off. "Are those for you, Beth? Or are you shopping for your grandmother?"

Now it wasn't just my cheeks on fire. It was my whole face. I said nothing. Because I was dying.

Elise took my nonresponse the way I should have known she would. "Really, Beth. You might want to invest in some thongs." She patted my arm in an almost motherly way. "They're a kind of underwear, not flip-flops. They're open in the ..." She actually started describing what a thong was to me.

I rolled my eyes, then wished I hadn't. I knew I could never get away with the stuff Ronnie did. "I know what thongs are."

"Oh. Sorry. I just assumed you didn't since you're buying ... those. I mean you do want to keep Rico interested, don't you?"

I was dying, still, but I found my voice enough to say, "Rico? Who's Rico?" I snuck a look at Junior. He'd stopped ringing and was listening intently to our conversation. I said, "Is there a problem?" He started ringing again, looking slightly guilty.

"Sorry." She didn't sound it. "I meant your husband. Obviously. Unless there's someone else you're trying to attract." Here she cast a look at Junior out of the corner of her eye.

I was beginning to stop dying. And moving into being really pissed. "His name is Rick."

"Well, I'm sure Rick would prefer something more ... interesting." Then to my horror she addressed Junior. "How about you? Does your girlfriend wear sexy underwear?"

"No comment, ma'am." I snuck another look at him. He looked like he was trying not to grin.

Elise, on the other hand, looked suddenly furious. It took me a few seconds to realize why. It was because he had called her "ma'am."

She was too cool to take her anger out on Junior or to let the look linger on her face. But it didn't take a genius to figure out who would face the brunt of her anger.

"Well. But just be honest." Elise was still talking to Junior to my huge mortification. "Would you go out with a girl who wore these?" She picked up the last pair of my underwear and held it up high for the world—at least the cheapo department store world—to see.

I snatched the pair out of her hands, barely able to contain my surging anger. I hoped Junior would just ignore her. But he looked me in the eye and winked. "Depends on the girl." Meanwhile I felt like my face might just combust from anger and embarrassment.

"Don't you need my credit card or something?" I asked Junior. I couldn't remember a purchase ever taking this long. That got him to remember his cashier duties, and finally, I paid and was out of there. But not before feeling like I'd been through one hugely horrific ordeal. All just to buy some panties.

CHAPTER TEN

THE WANNABE

So it had been a week since I opened my big freaking mouth and asked Ronnie the raging hormone question. Which was a mistake for at least two reasons. First, she never answered it, which was the whole point of my asking. And second, well, it was just a gut feeling that I'd made a mistake by choosing her as a confidant. Now it seemed so stupid to have done that. But, isn't that what friends do? Help each other? Ask for advice when needed? But maybe not in this group.

Amazingly, though, so far so good. No one had made any snide comments. And these women were queens of snide. I hoped and prayed that I was out of the woods.

When I pulled up to the bus stop and both Elise and Brad were present, along with everyone else, I got a sinking feeling in my stomach. In fact, for the first time in a long time I thought about not getting out of my car despite the fine weather.

I caught Elise looking over with a condescending smile. I got out.

Everyone ignored me at first, then nods and greetings all around. Brad's "Hi" included a strategically placed once-over that Elise missed.

Elise clapped her hands. "So, my social media request? I need a report from everyone." Shit. I'd forgotten.

Of course, she looked at me first. "Working on it," I replied, mustering a confident got-it-under-control tone.

She glared briefly then went on to her next victim.

Everyone answered something similar, except kiss-ass girl who had already done hers, probably the same day Elise mentioned it.

"Well, you slackers need to get up to speed." She shared a conspiratorial glance with Kelly. "I'd hate to have to put something out there that would be less than complimentary for you." She laughed without much humor. Shit. She was threatening to torment us using social media? Didn't she have enough ways already?

Brad spoke up. "Elise is pretty popular on social media. How many friends you have on Facebook again, babe? Five hundred?"

"No, babe. I've got many more than that." Her face showed her satisfaction at her impressive numbers, ones her own husband was unaware of. "I won't tell you the exact amount, look it up if you want to know." She paused. "But, I've always thought that was such a weird concept. Internet friends." She got a strange look, as if thinking about that phrase.

Brad laughed. "Yeah. Sort of like fake friends. You know all about those."

Her face got a dark look. She glared at Brad for a few seconds but then unexpectedly responded. "I might." Then, her eyes bored into each of us in turn as if trying to decide just who was the biggest fake. Her steely gaze had nothing on a bad cop during a shakedown.

Kelly was quick with a response. "You? Have fake friends? Impossible, girlfriend."

Other voices joined in to reassure her, including mine.

Ronnie ended the reassurance with a subject change. "So, Brad, to what do we owe the honor of your presence?" There was just a hint of sarcasm in her voice.

He shrugged. "Just hanging with the wife."

"Isn't he so sweet?" Elise slipped an arm around his waist and he promptly returned the favor. "Always wanting to be with me." She paused and shared a conspiratorial glance with Beth. Actually Beth. I couldn't remember that ever happening. Beth raised her brows, looking like she was also surprised.

Elise went on smoothly, "Especially since, from what I hear, I might have something to worry about. Competition wise. Because some women, some of my own friends possibly, at this time of life, they get kind of ..."

"Kind of ... what?" Brad prompted, sounding eager. As for me, I didn't want to hear anymore. In fact, I desperately wished I knew some way to stop this conversation. But what Elise wanted, she got. Especially if it involved embarrassing a friend. Or whatever it was we were to her.

Elise paused, looking like she was measuring her words. "I'm trying to think of a tactful way to put it. You know, their hormones rage." Here a look at me out of the corner of her eye.

Kelly chimed in. "Oh. You mean they're like horny all the time?"

"Precisely." Elise smiled like the Cheshire cat, looking me in the eye then. My stomach flipped and flopped like I was going into labor. My cheeks felt warm.

Brad cleared his throat. "Then it's the best time of life." Through my embarrassment I snuck a glance at him. But he wasn't looking at me. He was grinning while trying to catch Beth's eye, unsuccessfully. Suddenly my embarrassment faded and I got annoyed. Why was he looking at her?

Elise smirked. "Some women even take up with young

men. Teens even." She shook her head with disgust.

What did that mean? I'd never taken up with a teen. I glanced at her in annoyance. But she wasn't looking at me. Brad was still grinning, enjoying this conversation way too much. It was a relief when the bus finally came, and I could sulk off, tail between my legs.

Some friends I had. Some great fucking friends.

THE QUEEN BEE

I chatted with Kelly by my car, wondering if I should give her the heads-up. But then, why bother? I'd just wait and see her reaction along with the others. I could be patient. We talked of small, unimportant matters and then headed over to the others as usual.

Everyone was there except Gail, but she arrived soon, checking her watch like always and looking peeved. Well, girl, I felt like saying, Beth has clearly figured out one thing at least—getting here early is to her benefit. You'd think Gail could figure that out as well. Especially since she'd had longer to do her figuring.

I waited till the gang was all assembled to make my announcement. "So, ladies. We're doing things a little differently this Halloween."

I was met with a chorus of responses, everything from Ronnie's disinterested, "Oh?" to Kelly's eager, "Really? What is it?"

I smiled. "I decided since things are a bit different this year," here I broke off and looked at Beth out of the corner of my eye, "we should also move with the times. And in that vein, I'm choosing what everyone will be this year." I waited a beat. "Assuming of course that you're all okay with that." I didn't really think anyone would object—they'd better not if they knew what was good for them—but I threw that in to sound like I actually cared what they thought.

Gail looked confused. "But you already ..."

I gave her a look. "I mean the adults too." Really, I didn't think I'd have to spell that out.

"Oh, great!" Gail replied a bit too eagerly with Kelly quickly echoing her. But my eyes were on Beth. She was silent at first but when she realized I was waiting for her to respond, she put in, "Sounds good." I detected fear on her face before she masked it over and returned to a blank slate.

Ronnie's voice drew my attention to her. "So, what are you having us dress up as? Since the girls are princesses, are we going to be queens? Or evil stepmothers, perhaps?"

Did she sound a bit sarcastic when she said that? Was she implying something? I decided to let it go for now and continue with my announcement. "Actually, I thought it would be fun for us to be princesses, too. A great mother-daughter bonding opportunity. After all, soon they'll outgrow the princess craze and start into other less girly things. Jordan hates the princesses now." I wrinkled my nose. "So, we have to enjoy this time while it lasts."

Again, there was another chorus of cheers, my friends firmly supporting my idea. But my eyes were on Beth. I wanted to see that fear again. And I wasn't disappointed. It was there, albeit briefly, before she again got it under control.

Ronnie's voice again drew me back. "So which princesses are we going to be? Who am I?" She laughed.

"I have to tell you my heart is set on Mulan."

Mulan? No, I had something else chosen for Ronnie. And even if I hadn't, she wouldn't get that, especially not after telling me. She was usually smarter than that. Unless, it was just her way of giving me a clue of what someone else should be. I'd ponder that later.

"Well, Ronnie, part of the fun is that I'm not telling you what I've chosen until the day before. I thought I'd add some suspense and intrigue into the proceedings. Again, I hope that's okay with everyone." Again, I knew it would be.

Sure enough, my choir all agreed with me. But Gail looked a little confused. "But how will we order our costumes on such short notice?"

I rolled my eyes. Usually I disliked that gesture, favoring more subtle and less teenager-ish behavior. But really, Gail was making me wonder where she'd left her brain this morning.

Ronnie answered for me. "I take it you're ordering the costumes for all of us?"

I nodded and saw Gail's cheeks get more color. "You ladies can pay me back later." Oh, they'd pay alright. Big time.

Gail looked like she wanted to say something, but she kept quiet. This time Kelly spoke up. "So. I guess you know our sizes."

"Yes. I can judge pretty well, I think. None of us are plus size, heaven forbid. So, no worries on that account." They could worry plenty, but not about that.

Soon, we went our separate ways, and all things considered, I thought the Halloween announcement went well. And, I thought happily, this time even Ronnie would be in the dark. And no doubt wondering why I'd left her that way.

THE INFORMER

"So, she's choosing our costumes. For the first time, I take it. Why?"

Beth had a couple fine lines on her forehead I'd never noticed before. Not surprising. These women had that effect.

I pursed my lips, quickly picked up my coffee cup and drank deeply. I didn't want to admit that was the very question bothering me, along with the fact that she hadn't asked for my help this time. I wondered why she was cutting me out. "I don't know," I finally admitted. "But it's probably nothing to worry about."

Beth snorted. "Please. Remember who you're talking to. The woman whose chest blew up last time. I have plenty to worry about, thank you very much." Beth stared into her coffee cup with a funny expression, like she suddenly wondered if it had been poisoned.

"You can relax about that at least. Elise never does repeats. Too unoriginal. Especially ..." I trailed off, biting my tongue. I'd been about to say "especially someone else's prank," but that would have been incredibly stupid. One, Beth might not know it was a prank. And two, that would've made it sound like it wasn't Elise's idea. I hurried on. "I think it's just what she said. She wants to keep us guessing."

"And if we hate what she's chosen it'll be too late to get anything else."

"There's that too. Although, you could get something else now. But if you don't wear what she picked for you, then ..."

"There will be hell to pay."

"Right."

Jessie ran in. "Mommy, I want to know what I'm being for Halloween."

I sighed. "I've told you. It's a surprise."

"But ..."

"It's a princess. You know that."

She rolled her eyes to the ceiling. "I want to know which princess."

I smirked. "We all do."

"What?" Jessie looked confused.

"Nothing, hon."

Selena walked in and tugged on Jessie's shirt. "Come on, let's play."

"What about Selena? What princess ..."

"We don't know. Not for anyone. Not yet."

"But I want ..."

"Okay, Jessie. You know what? Why don't you ask Elise? Because the whole thing is her idea."

Jessie got quiet and pouty looking.

"What?" I asked the question, but I had a pretty good idea what the problem was.

"I'm not asking her," she said quietly.

"Why not?"

"She scares me." I raised my eyebrows. I hadn't expected her to say it straight out like that. I assumed it was something to that effect, but it still surprised and annoyed me to hear her say it so blatantly. I didn't want her to be scared of her. I wanted her to be stronger than that. But then, was that realistic?

"She scares me, too," Selena chimed in.

I met Beth's eyes briefly and we shared a nonverbal message. It was an echo of my former words. *We all do.*

THE TARGET

"So, ladies. I have a great idea. We're going to play How Young Are You? today." Elise's eyes danced with eager anticipation.

Coincidentally—or not—my stomach started dancing from something far less pleasant.

I glanced at Ronnie. She had on her poker face as usual. She avoided my eyes, which I found annoying. I glanced at all the others and, although it was far from obvious, I thought everyone else's anxiety went up a notch. Or two.

Kelly laughed, looking and sounding the least concerned. "What about How Hot Are You?"

Elise frowned slightly. "We'll do that one another day. So. Who's going first?"

I stared at the ground, feeling like a grammar school kid who hadn't done her homework. Or maybe a shy young kid who was scared to death of making a fool of herself in front of the class.

"Beth, I think ..." Elise trailed off and I gave in and looked at her, feeling my already funky stomach get funkier.

I waited for her to finish while she looked like she couldn't decide something. Finally she smiled. "I'll let you go last. Since you're new." The words might have been nice and friendly, but neither they nor the smile fooled me. But at least I was off the hook for the moment.

Elise turned to Gail, raising her perfectly manicured brows.

Gail looked at her hands and picked at a nail before looking up with determination. "Okay. Sure. I got this." It felt like a self-pep talk. "Uh. Let's see."

Elise frowned, looking impatient.

"Okay. I was buying a miniskirt, right? Which was just too cute, by the way. Anyway, Joe was with me and he's so clueless about fashion. He said in front of the salesman, 'I think a short skirt like that is for younger girls.' What a dork, right? But the salesman, who was young and hot, turns to me and says, 'If you don't mind my saying so, you can definitely pull it off.'"

Elise laughed and held out her hand for a high five. "Nice."

Kelly smiled but then said, "Salesmen are funny, aren't they? I mean they'll say anything to make a sale."

Gail shot Kelly a glare, which Elise missed since she was already turning to her next victim ... er, friend. This time it was Kelly in the hot seat. But she looked totally cool.

"Right. So the other day I was at that new Chinese restaurant. The one that just got its liquor license. And can you believe that I got carded?"

Elise laughed, did the high five again, looking even more pleased. "Sweet, Kel."

Gail smirked. "But were they carding everyone?"

Kelly sent Gail a sharp glance. "No. I'm sure they weren't."

But Elise had moved on to Ronnie. I started panicking. Because I was next in line. Even though I was starting to get the gist of this "game," I felt far from comfortable.

Ronnie still had her poker face. "Elise, you know this isn't my thing. But I'll play. So, a man came over to the house the other day to sell us some insurance."

She paused and looked at Kelly.

Elise laughed. "Insurance? Ronnie, why bother? Just buy it online, then you don't have to deal with those annoying salespeople." She wrinkled her nose.

"Ian is old school; he wanted to talk to the guy in person. His name is Blair Landon, if anyone wants a house call." She paused and eyed Kelly again. "Anyway, he's this older guy, probably in his sixties. And when he saw my daughter, he said something like, 'Oh, are you two sisters?' And he winked at me, like it was a great joke."

Elise gave a groan and a slight chuckle. "Okay, Ronnie. I'll let that go for today, but I think you can do better next time."

Elise looked at me now and my stomach dropped. "Um," I started, though I had no clue what was going to come out of my mouth next.

Unexpectedly, Elise said, "I'll go next, Beth. To give you more time." She turned to the others. "So, I was at the grocery store and I was buying kid stuff. You know popsicles, string cheese, and popcorn. And the young teen boy checking me out—no pun intended—asked me, 'Are you babysitting tonight?'"

We were all loud in our support, laying it on thick. Kelly was loudest, saying, "That is amazing, girlfriend. He thought you were a teenager."

Elise smiled with a look that passed for modesty.

Now it was my turn. I had no more "get out of jail free" cards. But before my stomach could take another plunge,

Elise surprised me again. "Beth, since you're new at this, I'd like to do you a favor."

"What do you mean?" She sounded friendly and helpful. I didn't trust her.

"Well, I imagine this is hard for you. To come up with something when you've never played before. So, if it's all right with you, I'll take your turn for you."

I realized later I misunderstood her. At the time, I thought she meant she would take another turn herself, even though she had just taken hers. I should have known that was not the case. So, even though I didn't trust her, I didn't understand how her taking my turn for me was going to hurt me. But it soon became clear. Crystal clear.

Taking my silence as sufficient encouragement, she began the humiliation. "Beth is so modest, she'd never tell you ladies this, but she also has a look that teen boys go for."

With that first sentence I could feel my cheeks flaming to life and my stomach dropping like a rock. It took everything I had to stand my ground, hold my head up, and plant a fake smile on my face.

"We both happened to be at Discount Mart, and ..."

Gail gasped.

Elise looked at her. "What?"

"I just ... um, didn't know you shopped there." She winced.

Elise glared. "I don't. I was just buying teacher gifts." She glared some more, seeming to forget her story.

"You were at Discount Mart ..." Kelly prompted.

Elise sent Gail one final glare. "Right. And Beth was buying these old-lady underpants. Honestly, Beth, what were you thinking? The higher end stores might be out of your sphere, but you didn't even consider Victoria's Secret?"

Gail giggled and looked at me. "Are you wearing them now?"

Kelly smirked. "We can pants her and see."

Pants me? Wasn't that a teenage boy prank? I mean how low could these women go? But I was pretty sure I already knew that answer. And it was rock bottom.

Elise sent a fake glare to Kelly. "Please, Kelly. You're scaring Beth. We're not animals. Anyway, the cashier was a young good-looking guy and remember Beth ..." She broke off and turned to me like I was actually enjoying this and wanted to hear the story again. "You remember what happened? I was asking him if he'd date a girl who wore those ridiculous things and he answered," she paused for effect, "'It depends on the girl.' Isn't that just so sweet? And then he winked at Beth."

She paused and everyone fake congratulated me. Elise turned to me and put a hand on my arm. "This teen boy must have thought Beth was a teen too, and even though she was buying old-lady panties, he still liked her. That's quite an accomplishment. So, let's hear it for today's winner!" She led them all in a round of applause.

The humiliation of hearing Elise tell that story with young Brian was bad enough. But then another concern came to me. Would she now want to get me back? Because even though she instigated it, she wouldn't like me being called the "winner." I feared it was all a set up to make me pay, yet again.

CHAPTER ELEVEN

THE QUEEN BEE

So. Since the Halloween party was still over a week away, I needed something else. Something to ease my weary mind. For whatever reasons, Brad's usual tricks weren't doing the job. Well, honestly, I've always been a woman who needs other diversions. Something besides what men alone can provide.

I needed, even craved, another good prank. So, I sent messages, both verbal and otherwise, to Ronnie, knowing they'd make contact. And now the place and the time were all set. It was to be a bit out of the ordinary this time. In more ways than one.

First the setting would not be my house. It would be at a school event. Usually I don't choose events like that, preferring to have total control, which is easier to obtain in my own home and with the people I choose to invite. But I decided to shake things up a bit and try something new.

Second, there were going to be two victims this time. And both would no doubt be caught off guard because it seemed like I'd already slammed them. But little did they know that was just the warm-up.

Ronnie had come through again, as usual. The woman missed her calling; she should have been a detective. But then surely this was more fun than solving murder mysteries. Frankly I'd been a bit worried about her. I knew, from what Gail told me, that Ronnie and Beth had been letting their daughters play together. I knew this was in part to get Beth back in our group, but she'd been back for a while, yet the play dates continued.

That fact bothered me a bit. Was Ronnie losing focus? Actually becoming friendly with Beth or allowing her daughter to be friendly with Selena? Some friendship in a group like this was inevitable and, on the surface anyway, the goal. But Ronnie had better not have forgotten the far more important goals of this, my posse.

I chose the internet to make the communication, using both Facebook and Instagram. I put messages out to everyone. "Tomorrow night, HS fundraiser. Must show. Hubbies 2, no kids. Dinner and lecture on how 2 keep our teens safe. After all, we can't be 2 prepared for those scary teen years."

In my case, because of Jordan, I was already there, but I didn't like to point that out. The others had more time since their kids were younger. I didn't like to be reminded that I had one of the oldest kids. Beth was the one exception; she was good for that at least since her son was a year older.

Everyone replied back and we were good to go. I rubbed my hands together with eager anticipation, barely avoiding foaming at the mouth. Maybe it was sad, but what Brad could do for me was nothing compared to the high I got from this.

THE INFORMER

I did what I do best. I found the dirt I needed to find, easily as usual, and then gave it back to her majesty. It was nothing new. Nothing I hadn't done many times before, too many times to count.

But for some reason it felt different this time. It was harder. Not the finding—that had been business as usual, requiring only a little digging. No, it was the giving that had been hard.

Was I changing in some fundamental way? Was I finally developing a conscience? And if so, was that a good thing or a bad thing? Or was it that I was starting to let friendship blind me to the whole reason I signed up for this?

I couldn't let myself forget the big picture. Why I was involved in the first place. It was for my daughter, to give her something that I didn't have. To give her a piece of the popularity pie, to allow her to rule her universe. Somebody would do it, and so why not my daughter? She was plenty deserving. Naturally, she wouldn't rule it alone. But she'd be one of the head honchos. That was surely worth the price. Wasn't it?

But if I messed up, if I didn't do my job, what then? What would that mean for Jessie? She'd be back to square one. Or maybe worse. Because how far would Elise go to get back at me should I fail? Would she only go after me? Or after Jessie too? I knew only too well what she was capable of.

No, failure was not an option. I was in too far and too deep. I had no choice but to keep going, to keep playing the game. Even if my newfound conscience—or maybe my heart—started to tell me otherwise.

THE WANNABE

I pulled into the high school parking lot for some stupid event that Elise wanted us to attend, a fundraiser for the high school. Even though I had no teens. What was up with that? Luckily I just happened to check Facebook earlier today. I didn't like to think what would've happened if I missed seeing her invite. Or more accurately, her summons.

At least I knew there'd be nothing more about my raging hormones. Elise never did a redo. It was always on to something new. And although I'd been mad at the time, now that it was over, I saw that I'd gotten off fairly easy. What had she done, after all? Only made some vague comments, in front of Brad, true, but he'd seemed oblivious to the fact it was me she was referring to. Really it had been mild. Maybe she was losing her touch? If so, I wouldn't complain.

I walked through the door and found the girls assembled in a circle in the lobby. Elise turned to me immediately. "Gail, I was afraid you didn't get my invite."

Her command, she meant. "I got it." And, I wasn't late. What was up with her always making it seem like I was chronically late?

"I'm so glad you did. You will be too, I'm sure." And she winked conspiratorially at me like we were in cahoots with each other. Right. I'd never been that far up the ladder.

Kelly snorted. "Look who's here. Well, Gail, at least you weren't last."

I sent her a glare, since Elise's eyes were on Beth walking through the door.

After greeting Beth, Elise said, "Well, ladies, let's go find our seats. Since this was rather last minute, we'll have to be at different tables. But ..." she broke off looking at me and Beth in turn, "I think you'll be pleased with the arrangements all the same." Did I just imagine the wicked gleam in her eye? I hoped so. Because that glance did not bode well for me. A wicked gleam? Far worse.

We wandered the banquet hall, searching for our names, since it was assigned seating. I'd checked every table but came up empty. All the others had found their tables. I started to feel panicky. Was this a prank? Maybe Elise had "forgotten" to give them my name so I'd end up sitting on the floor. Well, there was one empty table toward the back, but it had no nametags on it. Maybe that was the plan. For me to end up sitting alone.

I headed toward the empty table when I realized there was one table I hadn't checked. It had appeared full at first glance so I had quickly dismissed it. Now I wandered toward it. Maybe there were some empty seats there after all.

There was one seat. And sure enough, it was my name on the tag. I glanced around at my table mates and saw they were all guys. Good-looking—actually studly—guys. They all looked up as I approached, several grinning. A particularly hot guy looked me in the eye and winked. "Will you be joining us? What a pleasure."

They all stood up and waited for me to sit down. I got the sinking feeling that this was a setup. And that the worst was still to come. I could feel the warmth spreading up from my neck like some strange and nasty disease. If only it were. Then maybe it would have the power to finish me off.

Something made me look over at Elise. She was grinning like the Cheshire cat. No—make that like a tiger just before the kill.

THE TARGET

"I'm done, Ronnie. That's it. The jig is up." I stood in Ronnie's driveway. Selena was already in the car, no doubt tired from her long day and school followed by the play date. I was tired too—of all the tricks and pranks associated with this clique.

Ronnie stood with her arms crossed. "You can't be done. It's impossible."

"Oh it's very, very possible. It's a done deal. I am out of this freaking clique." To hell with that other reason. I'd take my chances.

"That would be suicide."

What did that mean? "Sorry?"

"You probably are sorry that you joined up with us. God knows, some days I am, too." I thought she looked suddenly tired too, and older somehow.

"I meant why ..."

"Why would it be suicide? Simple. You're in too far. You can't go home again, Beth. Forget Kansas. It's the Emerald City forever. For better or worse." She paused. "For both of us."

"Uh, Ronnie? You're kind of scaring me." I frowned. "And why the Wizard of Oz analogy?" I paused. "Although I guess I see it. With all the wicked witches."

"I hope you don't consider me one." She had her usual blank look on her face. "Okay, I'll choose another comparison. Hotel California?"

"Um … I can never leave?"

"Bingo."

"What about killing the beast?"

She did a half-snort, half-laugh. "Not likely." She got a curious expression on her face as she stared off into space. "Yet strangely tempting."

"But why can't I leave?"

"She won't let you. Not now. You know too much—about her, her ways, her friends. And then too, she likes you."

I stared at Ronnie like she'd lost her last brain cell.

"In her sick, twisted way, yes, she likes you. Like a cat likes a favorite toy mouse."

"I'm her favorite punching bag? What about Gail?"

"She likes you both. For similar reasons."

"Why the hell couldn't you have told me this the last time? When I left and you brought me back?"

She shrugged, still looking tired but now a bit sorry too. "I guess I just … liked you too. For less sick and twisted reasons." She gave me a weak smile.

I sighed heavily. "But what could she do to me? I mean that she hasn't already done?"

Ronnie gave me a look. "Do I really have to answer that? So far she's been only playing and look what she's done. If she gets really pissed, trust me, you do not want to see what she's capable of."

"But … there has to be a way out."

"If you find one, let me know. Maybe I'll go with you."

Annoyed, I left her and walked to my car. I got in and drove home, but although Selena got out and ran inside, I just sat there. And my brain went back to that event at the high school, causing me to relive the latest horror show that was my life.

That night, I'd found my table and at first everything seemed okay. Rick was with me, so I considered myself lucky—some of the women were separated from their spouses.

Then the man to my right turned to me and I suddenly got a funny feeling that I wasn't—lucky, that is. "Hello." He held out his hand, "Brian Peters." He paused, giving me an assessing look. "You look familiar. Do we know each other?"

I couldn't answer. I was too busy dying. Because it was Junior's dad—the boy I'd made a fool out of myself with. Twice.

He went on before I could answer. "Oh. That's right. Tina told me I went to school with someone at my table. But I don't remember your name."

As I looked at the man before me, I was struck at how stupid I'd been to mistake the boy for his dad. Where the boy was dreamy, the dad was well, a nightmare. He bore little resemblance to the hunky guy he'd been back in the day. Now he was a good fifty pounds heavier, well on his way to losing his hair, and his teeth had the yellow stains of a smoker. Odd to think that while Brad had found the Fountain of Youth, this guy had aged in record time.

I realized he was waiting for me to give my name. I wanted to give him a fake one, but Tina, the organizer of this event, obviously knew me, so there was no choice but to admit the truth.

"It's Beth Tapia."

"Oh, ah, I don't remember ..."

"Winters was my maiden name."

"Oh. That's right." Clearly he still had no clue who I was. And that was fine by me. I prayed Junior hadn't told his dad the little story about me.

He stared at me, obviously still trying to place me. And failing. "We took shop together, right?"

"Yes. Exactly." Shop? What girls took shop? I wanted to say we'd been in home ec class together. This was back when the school system was gender challenged.

"See? I do remember you." He looked smug.

I fought to keep from rolling my eyes. "Impressive."

I breathed a sigh of relief as he disengaged from me and took up with someone on his right. But then a familiar voice stopped all conversation at the table.

"Dad, you took my car keys." I glanced over and saw my worst nightmare—Junior.

Oh, damn. I stared straight ahead and kept completely still. As if that would somehow make me invisible.

"No, I didn't." Brian Sr. reached in his pocket and pulled out some keys. He chuckled. "That's odd, I don't remember taking them. Sorry, son. How did you get here, anyway?"

"Got a ride from Nick. But I need my keys, Dad." He sounded annoyed. I didn't look anywhere remotely near him.

"Here you go." Junior started to walk away. "Wait, Brian. Since you're here, I'd like to introduce you around."

Great, just great. He has to go and do the proud father routine. Brian Sr. went around the table naming us for his annoyed and impatient son. When he got to me, I cringed inwardly and avoided Junior's eyes.

"I'm sorry. What was your name again?" Brian Sr. was nothing if not predictable.

"Beth." I looked briefly at Junior then and saw he recognized me. Like I knew he would. He nodded, giving me an inside joke kind of smile that unfortunately his father caught. They shared a look and some meaning seemed to pass between them. That wasn't good, either.

Junior left and I looked toward Rick, but he'd gotten up to get a drink. I hoped Brian Sr. would go back to treating me like he did in high school. I wanted to be ignored now. But I'm the type who rarely gets what I want.

He leaned toward me, a lazy smile on his face. "So. Beth."

I raised my brows, saying nothing.

"I won't forget your name anymore. Trust me." He was speaking only slightly above a whisper.

"I'm sorry?"

"Look, my son told me what happened, so you don't have to play dumb. Or feel bad. I get this kind of stuff a lot. All the chicks liked me back in the day. I couldn't date everyone." He paused and reached in his pocket. "Here's my card. Call me sometime. I'd be happy to make it up to you."

"Make what up to me?" My face was on fire. I was pretty sure I knew what he meant.

"For ignoring you back in high school." He leered at me. "Come see me. I promise I won't ignore you now."

"I see you two are reliving old times. Beth, this must be such a ... treat for you." I looked up to see Elise grinning—need I add, evilly.

I knew two things then. One, she'd seen and heard a good part of what happened. But two, and more importantly, somehow the whole thing had been her doing.

THE WANNABE

Elise had us all go to her house today after we got the girls off the bus. For the grand unveiling. To find out, finally, what costumes she chose for us. I didn't like it. I wanted to choose my own. I mean, I built a name for myself based on fashion, didn't I? But then, she took one of fashion's biggest nights, at least in the young mom–daughter world, all to herself. And with it, all the glory.

I didn't want to go for other nonfashion reasons. Actually, I wanted to be anywhere else. I still couldn't believe how she'd slammed me at that fundraiser. Made me sit with a bunch of stud muffins. Yeah, it might not seem like a punishment; in fact, maybe I would have enjoyed it under other circumstances. But it was obvious soon after my sitting down that not only did Elise organize the table arrangements but my tablemates knew. I mean they were in on the joke. Based on comments they made and the looks they were giving me, it was clear Elise had spilled my secret to them. And how mortifying was that?

By the end of the night, I'd been propositioned several times and had to listen to double entendres of the lewdest kind. I don't usually embarrass easily, but in this situation it was impossible to not feel like a freaking idiot. Or worse, a skanky slut. Especially when Elise came over to gloat and rub in the embarrassment with some below-the-belt comments of her own. And then, I knew Joe had heard a few of the comments and I wondered what he thought. He'd said nothing but I noticed his raised eyebrows a couple times.

Almost as bad as Elise's enjoyment of my misery was the knowledge of just who backstabbed me. I was pissed at Ronnie but even more so at myself. Because I'd been incredibly stupid to trust that snake. Never again would I be that naïve. To think I actually thought she was nice and friendly. Yeah. Friendly like a Rottweiler.

But I had no choice. I was stuck with them, just as surely as if they were quicksand. Actually, in many ways they were. I was sinking all the time, losing more and more of myself with each year I hung out with them.

But knowing that didn't mean I could walk away from them. I couldn't. Not now. Not after all I'd invested in this group. So, I never had any choice. To the stupid princess announcement I went.

After ushering us all in with fake warmth, Elise handed us each a piece of paper with our chosen princess written on it, in gold lettering printed on fancy, floral stationary. Had to give it to Elise—she did nothing half-ass or less than classy. Mom and daughter would be going as the same princess. We were told to keep it secret from each other if possible, but I wondered if the girls could pull that off.

I held my piece of paper in my hands, taking a deep breath. I just prayed I got a fashionable princess. That's all I really cared about. I mean I liked pretty clothes. I didn't want to dress like a freaking geek or an old lady. But then all the princesses were fashionable, right? I had nothing to worry about.

But when I opened my paper I almost swore out loud. Because I was Mulan. Freaking Mulan. The princess that goes to war, dressed like a guy. What was Elise thinking? This was the only princess I didn't want to be. In fact, I'd forgotten all about her. She wasn't even a princess in my book. But then I remembered Ronnie saying she wanted to be Mulan. Had she set me up? Was that Ronnie's little code way of letting Elise know the very princess I hated? It was very possible. Compared to what she'd already done, that would be too easy.

Suddenly I realized I needed to look happy. I pulled out my biggest smile and then looked around. And saw lots of other big, exaggerated smiles. Were others in the same boat as me? Or were they actually happy? I sort of guessed the second, because I'd already been given the worst. What did they have to complain about? They had freaking Belle and Cinderella. Not Tomboy War Girl.

Then I remembered Nina. Poor Nina. Would she be crushed? After glancing around, I spied her dancing about, chatting happily with her friends. I assumed she didn't open her paper, but then she came over and whispered in my ear, "I'm Mulan. Isn't that cool?" I forced myself to nod in reply.

Well, one of us was happy at least. And after all, Halloween is all about the kids. Why did I always have to remind myself of that fact?

Elise suddenly drew all of our attention. "Ladies, now that you've all seen who you're dressing up as, I just want to point out what should be obvious, but may not be." She shot me a look out of the corner of her eye.

"As we all know, what is a princess without her prince? Therefore, your husbands will be dressing as your male counterparts. Just so you know I did take into account physical attributes when deciding who a couple would go as. For some of you this was obvious." She broke off and looked briefly at Beth, who I thought looked kind of shell shocked yet was trying to cover it up. "But for others it required a little more thought." She paused. "So, I hope everyone's happy. I want you all to know I worked hard to see to that."

We all thanked her and assured her that, yes, we were happy. Ecstatic even. Even as I pictured Joe, plump and jolly Joe, who'd be more at home in a Santa suit than a Chinese manly man getup. He'd look nothing like the hottie Mulan hooks up with.

I tried to find a bright side to all of this. All I managed to come up with was that I'd get some experience learning how to act the opposite of how I feel. Something told me this was a skill I'd need even more in the future.

THE TARGET

After dinner, I slipped into the bathroom with my costume. I put it on. And cringed. And felt like crying. Or stringing up a rope. Or maybe both. No, no, scratch that. I was tougher than that. At least, I thought I was.

Selena and I were going as Jasmine. Selena was thrilled. I was nauseated. I'd been nauseated since I'd opened the paper at Elise's house. But in front of them I'd forced myself to smile. To say I was happy. Because that's what you do when you're in this group. You grovel and lie a lot. And pretend to be something you're not. Come to think of it, that last part is what Halloween is all about. Only in this group, you live it every day.

I examined myself in the mirror, wondering why Elise had picked this for me. One reason I could guess all too easily. She'd even hinted at it herself, just in case I was too obtuse to get it. Clearly Jasmine, and her 'prince' Aladdin, had the requisite physical characteristics that also belonged to my husband. It was like she was saying, "Your hubby's got darker skin, so I'll make you two be the Arabian couple." Only I was actually pretty pale and had the wrong hair color. But Elise had thoughtfully provided a black wig that would cover my light-brown hair. I was surprised she didn't also include some spray tan.

And that brought me to the second reason, which was showing lots of skin. Did Elise pick this because she knew, or suspected anyway, that walking around in what was almost a bikini top would be hell for me, especially in that group? I mean I got the skimpiest princess except for maybe Ariel. But why Elise would want any of us to wear costumes showing a lot of skin was beyond me. Didn't she have any idea what Brad was like? Why give him any eye candy? Not that I really qualified as that, not compared to his wife. But still, why? At the thought of Brad seeing me in this, my nausea reached epic proportions.

Suddenly there was pounding on the bathroom door. "Mom, where are my shin guards?"

I groaned. "Ricky, they're in the closet downstairs."

"Nope. I looked."

"That's where they are. Just look again."

"Mom, will you just get them for me? Because Zach is waiting outside."

"Give me a minute to change."

"Mom. I don't have a minute. I need them now." Who knew a teenage boy could sound so whiny?

"Go ask your dad."

"He's outside talking to some guy. Please?"

I signed loudly. I took a towel and wrapped it around my shoulders and then walked out. Ricky gave me a funny look. "Mom, what are you wearing?"

"Never mind." My tone must have shown I was in no

mood.

I marched past him and went downstairs, annoyed with him and all guys everywhere for being so clueless at finding things. Kneeling down, I dug in the back of the closet and pulled out the shin guards. Ricky took them with a sheepish look. As I stood up, the towel fell from my shoulders.

Ricky gave me a funny look. "Ah, Mom. You look …" he trailed off, looking uncomfortable.

Suddenly a little voice chimed in, "Pretty. She looks pretty." I looked down and saw Selena beaming up at me. She looked so earnest that I bent down and gave her a hug.

I stood up again and I was suddenly looking into a different Rick's eyes—senior. He stared at me, clearly fighting a grin. It took me a second to realize that some guy I never saw before was standing next to him. Swell. Just invite all the neighbors in to see me in this ridiculous getup.

Rick picked up Selena. "You're right, Selena. Mommy looks muy linda."

Selena nodded.

Rick cleared his throat. "Beth, I'd like you to meet Dax Smith. Dax, this is my wife, Beth." Now his grin won. "But we like to call her Jasmine."

Chapter Twelve

THE INFORMER

So, Elise's chosen costume for me wasn't Mulan. I knew it wouldn't be; after all, reverse psychology is a way of life in this group. Or is it simply that what you say you want you never get? Not from Elise, anyway. And not often in life either.

Actually, I wasn't sure why I blurted that out. Had I been trying to set someone else up? It was a safe bet that Gail didn't want to be Mulan. Not a fashionista like her. And by casually mentioning Mulan, I was reminding Elise of that lesser-known princess. Maybe you could put it stronger, that I was planting the seed, since Elise was used to reading my clues, both verbal and non. And then doing with them what she chose, but usually not for good.

Yet, strange as it might be, that hadn't been my thought process at the time, although maybe backstabbing had become so ingrained that I did it on autopilot. But actually, other thoughts had been in my head. Other, strangely altruistic, thoughts. I'd remembered that Beth said her favorite princess was Mulan. And it was also a safe bet that while Gail would hate her, Beth would welcome her even had she not been her favorite. Mulan was the most—how to say it—covered princess. She was the non-skimpy one, which Beth would no doubt like.

So, by saying it, I'd been trying to plant a different seed but for a far-from-usual reason. There was a good chance that Elise would use the bait in that way. I guessed Elise wouldn't mind Beth wearing the frumpiest princess costume. So, it seemed a win–win situation. I marveled at my strange thoughts. Had I actually been trying to help someone? It was almost mind-boggling.

With all these thoughts in my head, I almost forgot about which princess Elise had chosen for me. But Jessie came running in to remind me. "Mommy, we're Belle. Isn't it great? That's who I wanted to be. Even Brianna said it would be perfect for me. Since I read so much."

I forced myself to smile. "Yes, hon. It does seem very appropriate."

She looked confused. "Appropriate? What does that mean ... wait, don't tell me. I want to guess."

I smiled, for real this time.

"Does it mean like it fits?"

I smiled bigger. "Yes. Exactly."

She ran off again, smiling from my praise. But my own smile faded. I couldn't explain why exactly, but I wasn't thrilled to have been chosen as Belle. On the surface it did seem perfect—she was the reading princess, you could almost say the smartest princess, but something about it bothered me. Maybe it was that it was too perfect. Maybe it was that I suspected Elise was with this choice somehow digging the knife in my back. Some kind of inside joke. Like, yeah, Ronnie's kind of off, not really one of us, so let's give her the beautiful yet slightly flaky princess. Did the song not say "a most peculiar mademoiselle"?

And then there was the whole beast thing. She'd said that she took into account physical attributes of both partners when considering her choice. Was she therefore saying something about my husband? Something far from complimentary? I was well aware that Ian was no Brad, but then I didn't particularly want him to be. I liked a man

I could trust—a faithful, honest, sincere man who would always be there for me. I pushed aside that nagging question of whether I deserved him or not. Fate had allowed me such a man. And I wouldn't screw it up.

I mean, so what if he'd never appear on the cover of *GQ*? There were, after all, more important things in life. And looks faded eventually. Someday, though it was hard to imagine now, even Brad would look old. He couldn't hold on to that Fountain of Youth forever. No one could. Not even Elise herself.

So fine, Elise. Enjoy your little joke. But we'll see who'll be laughing in about thirty years.

THE SIDEKICK

Two words. Snow White. Or maybe three words. Snow Freaking White. If you look at the princesses—I mean all the princess gear of which there is a ton of in my house, the three main babes are Cinderella, Belle, and Aurora, AKA Sleeping Beauty. But do I get any of those? No. I get the one who is sometimes included. Sometimes she's there in the background, eating an apple or something. And don't even get me started on that ugly dress of hers. Plus, she's the least attractive princess of the bunch. I don't even have black hair. So now I'm going to have to wear that nasty wig she got me which stinks. I like my own curls, thank you very much.

I would have preferred Cinderella. But I think we all knew who that will be. She may try to keep it as a big surprise, but that is just too obvious. Even without a costume, Elise is Cinderella. Looks-wise anyway, not personality wise. Cinderella was nice and generous—almost ridiculously nice given how badly she was treated. But Elise? Please. No one would ever dream of making her scrub floors.

No, Elise never even had to work for a living. When you're rich and beautiful, I guess life is always easy. Therefore she couldn't understand people less fortunate than herself. Why we have to make the choices we do. Why we can't just spend our days in comfort and luxury, killing time by playing pranks and engaging in mind games consisting mainly of one-upmanship.

Speaking of mind games, I knew, thanks to those not-so-subtle hints from Ronnie a while back, that she knew my secret. What I'd feared had happened. And I'd been in this group long enough to know what that meant. That day, she was only alerting me that I was busted; she wasn't telling on me. Yet.

She would choose the best time to strike—the best time to create the most favorable circumstance for herself. Or, she would use this to better her own position after some fall from grace. I had no doubt the truth about my job would come out, I just didn't know when. And, based on what I knew about Elise, it wouldn't go over well. Would she demote me from my privileged place because of it? I wasn't sure, but it was all too possible. She'd sought revenge for far lesser reasons.

Oddly though, despite these worries, I felt pretty calm. There was no sense stressing over any of this—either about Ronnie knowing my secret or about being forced to be Snow White. The situation was what it was. I would be Snow White for better or worse—I had no choice. I would have to deal with Ronnie at some future point, which might be, metaphorically speaking, my poisoned apple. At least I had done some planning; I had some tricks up my sleeve. I wasn't without options.

I just hoped Elise wouldn't serve apples at her party. Because I refused to play the idiot and bob for them.

THE QUEEN BEE

I lay down, waiting for Brad to come to bed, and thinking over the events of the evening. I'd unveiled my picks to the girls tonight. Tomorrow, Saturday night, was the party. Halloween was on Sunday this year so interestingly my party was on mischief night. I couldn't help but be proud and happy about that fact. It was like the calendar was my friend, this one time anyway. Usually it's just a reminder of passing time and that's no woman's friend. But now it seemed like all the forces were coming together to help make this a perfect evening.

I decided to have the party at my house after all. What can I say? I like control, and even though I'd have a lot at Kelly's, I wanted and needed more. Kelly looked a little ticked when I told her, but too bad. This was always my party. My choice and my rules, which she should know by now.

I think, judging by everyone's reaction, that I achieved what I wanted to achieve. Of course, it's tricky to judge because everyone is trying to look pleased. But if you look closely you can see other emotions there below the surface. Fear, anxiety, and even anger were present in varying degrees in all the women. Which is really what I was going for.

And now at the party tomorrow, the show will begin in earnest. I predict a smashing success. In fact, I'll accept nothing less.

Brad was still not coming to bed. Where was he? I walked out of the room and searched the house, but I couldn't find him anywhere. Finally I saw a note on the kitchen table, written in his annoyingly messy scrawl. "Went out for drinks with Steve. Be back soon." He didn't sign his name. No love. No X's or O's. It made me mad.

Not just the note, but its contents. Drinks with Steve? Why didn't he bring me? And why go out this late at night? He knew I hated this kind of thing. Which is why he snuck out and left this lame note.

I went to the door and peeked out. I'm not sure what I was looking for but what greeted my eye was Steve pulling their garbage can back to the house. Steve. Walking in his driveway. So, Steve was not out for drinks. Which begged the question: Who was my husband having drinks with? And why had he lied?

I wish I hadn't peeked outside. I wish I'd stayed in bed. Because not only are some questions better left unanswered, some are better left dead and buried.

***

Mischief night. A night made for mischief. Before what happened last night I might have—no definitely would have—enjoyed those words. But now I had to push from my mind a particular kind of mischief that filled me with uneasiness.

I hadn't waited up for Brad last night. I took a sleeping pill and went to bed. I wouldn't give him the satisfaction of acting like I was worried. I'd keep up the pretense. I was excellent at doing just that. Pretense was one of my specialties.

I stared at my reflection in the entryway mirror. A born Cinderella, yes, there was no denying the truth of that statement. The costume fit perfectly, so perfectly in fact that I could have worked at Disney, despite being older—I wouldn't say how much older—than most of those girls. Normally, that fact would have cheered me. After last night, I found it didn't give me the same shot of joy. Now, I wondered whether I should have picked a different princess. Maybe one showing more skin? Maybe that would make Brad happy and away from whatever kind of mischief he might be indulging in, mischief I didn't want to think about.

The next few minutes were a whirlwind of arriving guests. It was all so déjà vu. Kelly and Steve came first, Kelly looking almost silly in the Snow White getup. Really that dress was ugly. What were the princess-powers-that-be thinking when they designed it? However, the dress did suit my purposes. It showed her pretty plainly just what her place was. That she could never outdo me. And the black wig did not become her. She was much better suited to her auburn hair, which I happen to know she colored. Steve, conversely, looked quite the prince in his costume. I gave him a kiss, perhaps a bigger one that usual, but I just couldn't help myself. I made sure Brad was watching, but when I looked again he'd looked away.

The men had actually figured into my plan. I wanted to make the women look bad or feel as uncomfortable as possible while making the men look good. For some spouses that was a challenge indeed or, in Ronnie's spouse's case, damn near impossible, which is why I went with the beast. I worked with the raw material given to me and made the best of things.

The next guests to arrive were Ronnie and family. Ronnie looked pretty in her Belle dress and her face was the placid, usual expression that told you little or nothing. But I knew Ronnie, with her smarts and her habit of thinking through all scenarios, would understand my meaning. She'd get the joke and be annoyed with it.

Soon Gail and Joe showed in their Mulan getups. This one had required the least thought. Clearly, Gail would hate Mulan, and even now with a smile on her face I could still read her barely concealed annoyance. Joe looked silly in his getup, but not as silly as I thought. The outfit concealed a lot and therefore almost became him.

I assumed Beth would be late, like last time, wanting to postpone the torture. I knew she'd hate that skin-showing costume and relied on the fact that her discomfiture would likely undo any attractiveness of the getup. Add to that the fact that she was the least attractive one of us, she was the least worrisome one to have a sexy costume. I had avoided Ariel altogether, not wanting to have some other women dressed in that getup.

I was surprised when Beth and her street rat arrived on the tails of Gail and Joe. I'd told her they could bring their older boy too, although I had hoped they wouldn't. But I couldn't make it sound like that, so I'd included him in the invite. But now I saw him behind his father, looking annoyed and bored. I'd have to make sure Jordan kept away from him.

My eyes went back to Beth. I hurried over to her, eager to watch her squirm.

"Beth, let me take your coat." I thought she'd cling to that thing like a safety raft, but instead she shrugged it off and handed it over, looking unconcerned. But unconcerned was not the only thing she looked. I saw, with a sinking feeling in my stomach, that she looked good. Really good. The costume fit her like a glove, showing off curves that were usually well hidden. It got quiet—too quiet—and when I looked around the room, practically every man was staring at her, including Brad. Rico's hand slipped around his wife's waist, like a universal signal to the other males to back off.

Ronnie walked over to us. "Beth, how are you?" They air kissed. While they chatted, I pulled Beth's husband away.

"Rico. Let me look at you." I gave him a prolonged once-over. "You are too good to be true. A perfect Aladdin." I wasn't just saying it. Suddenly I thought tall, dark and handsome had definite advantages. I gave him a kiss. Again, I might have gone overboard a bit. But again, when I looked at Brad afterwards, he wasn't paying attention. Not to me anyway. He was still looking at Beth.

My eyes went back to Rico. I thought he had a funny look on his face. But he answered me smoothly enough. "And you're a perfect Cinderella, Elise."

"Brad. Get Rico a drink, will you?"

Brad looked confused. "Who's Rico?"

Oh, right. His name wasn't actually Rico, I guess he called himself Rick. But I would bet anything his actual name wasn't Rick or Richard. Must have been Ricardo or some such.

I laughed then and smoothed over my rare mistake. "I just decided to give Rick a little pet name. I only do that when I care enough to bother. So it's a compliment." I winked at Rick.

I caught Brad smirking, but after I glared at him he turned to Rick. "Okay, come on, Street Rat, let's get wasted."

Rick looked back at Beth with a slightly worried expression.

"Don't worry. I'll take care of Beth for you." I sure would.

He nodded and followed after Brad.

Well, I thought to myself, only one out of five, including my costume, was a dud. I suppose those weren't horrible odds. But not up to my usual standards either. So, I spent too much of that night stewing over things—how good Beth looked and how distracted Brad seemed, that I couldn't even enjoy the things that had gone well. And then, still later, I again drank too much wine for the second time in as many parties. Surely that wasn't a good sign.

THE TARGET

I chatted with Ronnie, watching Rick walk away with a funky feeling in my stomach. I'd asked him to stick to me like glue for the night, yet already he was leaving me. Great. Some help he was. And what was up with that kiss Elise gave him? I knew she gave her friends' husbands little peck-type kisses sometimes, but that was not a little peck.

Having Rick with me had enabled me to calmly hand my coat to Elise with no visible embarrassment over my lack of coverage. Well, that and the fact that I'd consumed a bit of liquid courage at home—nothing much. I didn't want to show up at the party drunk or who knew what might happen, especially due to a certain someone who lurked in bathroom doorways, ready to strike. But I just needed a little something to get me through this "happy" event.

Elise came over then, insisting that Ronnie and I go with the other women to have some ladies' drinks. Our daughters were already downstairs in the playroom, having their own little party, and I both guessed and hoped they were having more fun. My baby was with my parents for the night, although I now wished I had her here. It would be a reason to be less social.

Speaking of that, I didn't know what Ricky was supposed to do, but I saw that her older daughter had a few friends over and they were hanging out in the family room. I peeked in and saw both girls and boys. Ricky rolled his eyes but headed off to join them.

Soon Rick and Brad were back with beers in their hands, finding us women in the living room. Rick walked directly to my side. I breathed a sigh of relief.

Brad walked over to us, holding out some kind of mixed drink to me. "Beth, why don't you try this?" I reached out to take hold of it. "It's Sex On The Beach." He grinned as I nearly dropped the thing. "Whoa, there. You got it?" He was still grinning.

I looked away from him and sipped the drink. Rick turned to me. "Do you like it?"

I could sense Brad's smirk. I kept my eyes on Rick's. "Not particularly."

Brad chuckled. "Beth, you wound me. You liked it the last time. I mean the last time you had drinks over here."

Right. We never had drinks last time.

Brad turned to Rick. "Hey, you didn't make the last party. What happened? Beth told me it was because you have some lawn issues." Brad made it sound like these "lawn issues" were of a much more personal nature. "I told her I could hook her up. Cuz I don't have any issues. Lawn or otherwise."

Rick stared at him and I could tell he didn't know what to make of Brad. Just when the silence started to feel awkward he answered, "I have no issues either. Trust me." Rick looked him in the eye. Although he had a pleasant smile on his face, his eyes were hard. I guessed he wasn't talking lawn care either.

Brad smiled easily. "Well, it can happen to the best of us. Take Ian, for example. The guy has all kinds of issues. Crab grass, grubs, you name it. Finally he had to call in some heavy guns to kill all that shit."

I glanced over at Ian, really hoping for his sake that Brad actually meant his lawn this time. The conversation lagged then. I waited for Brad to walk away. But he wasn't done.

"So, Rick. I was wondering. Since I'm offering to hook you up maybe you can return the favor." He gave Rick a meaningful look. But from Rick's blank face, I could tell he had no clue what Brad was talking about. I didn't either. I just hoped it had nothing to do with me.

Rick raised his eyebrows. "I don't follow you."

"Oh, come on. Do I have to spell it out?"

"Yeah. I think you do." I could hear some annoyance in my husband's voice. Steve and Kelly walked up to us just then.

Brad slapped Steve on the back. "Well, you know what

they say about cops having the best dope. It's true." Brad laughed hard at his own joke, but Steve looked unnerved. Like Brad had spilled stuff he shouldn't have. Brad went on, oblivious to Steve's discomfort. "I'm guessing with your connections you could really hook us up."

"Connections?" There was now no mistaking the annoyance I heard in Rick's voice. "I don't ..."

But Kelly cut him off. "Brad, he's from Ecuador. Not Columbia."

I couldn't help speaking up because I finally saw where Brad was headed and I could barely believe how stupid he was. "I doubt all Columbians are involved in the drug trade." I turned to Brad. "But Rick *can* hook you up, Brad. If you need some blankets or wool sweaters, he's your man." I suppressed a smirk. It was totally unlike me to be dissing Brad. Maybe I had more alcohol at home than I realized.

Brad just looked confused, then kind of silly. "Oh. Well anyone could make that mistake."

Kelly rolled her eyes and we shared what almost passed for a sympathetic glance. She and Steve wandered off. I waited for Brad to do the same.

Finally he took the hint. Rick and I shared a look. He started to say something, but I put a finger to my lips. You don't talk about these people. Not where you might be overheard.

The next hour or so passed with social drinking, social pretending, and games, including bobbing for apples. Elise made Kelly go first over her strong opposition. All the men teased her for being a wimp. Her husband was one of the worst, saying, "Kel, you're acting like they poisoned the apples or something." He paused, laughing. "That's why

I'm here, right? Your own Prince Charming who can wake you up with a kiss."

"That was Sleeping Beauty, you doofus." Steve frowned, clearly not happy to be called doofus.

"Snow White also gets woken up with a kiss." Elise was stifling a grin as she gave her friend that helpful bit of trivia.

"Oh." Kelly looked silly.

Brad smirked. "Don't worry, Snow. If it's another Prince Charming you're looking for, I'm available." Steve laughed but I thought he sounded a little strained.

At some point—both time and the sequence of events became blurry, even though I tried to just sip that Sex On The Beach thing—Rick was suddenly not by my side. I looked around and all the men were missing. Some guy bonding going on perhaps?

I wandered over to the women hoping to get close to Ronnie, but all the women were in a tight circle formation, laughing and talking with animation, yet not loud enough for me to hear unless I was in their circle. I stood awkwardly by for a while, but a gap never opened, and I sensed I'd be doomed to remain on the wings.

I decided to find the bathroom. It would be something to do at least. But after wandering off I suddenly remembered the last time I found a bathroom in their house. But it would look too weird to go back into the room I just left. So, I resolved to find the main bathroom, steering clear of the one I'd used last time.

I found it and adjusted my wig and costume, trying to make the small amount of fabric give me the most possible coverage. When I figured I couldn't hide any longer, I opened the door, cautiously. I breathed a sigh of relief. No

Brad. I headed down the hall. When I got to the end, a door opened.

It was him. I tried to get by, but he blocked my path. The funkiness in my stomach returned tenfold.

"Hey, Jasmine." He laughed. "Don't look so spooked, babe. I'm not Jafar. Prince Charming means you no harm."

I laughed at his joke and tried to look unconcerned. "Doesn't Prince Charming want his Cinderella?"

"Actually, Cinderella asked me to find you. It seems your street rat spilled some chili sauce on his costume. Since you know his taste, she wanted you to choose a shirt for him to borrow from me."

It sounded wrong but before I knew it, he grabbed my arm and pulled me toward the door he'd just left. In my alcohol induced haze I wasn't thinking or acting fast or I would have tried to leave. I heard him make a low whistling noise as we walked through the doorway. I headed to the closet, wanting to get this over with.

I heard the door shut and the sound of the lock clicking into place. I looked over my shoulder. Brad was standing by the door, grinning.

That funkiness in my tummy felt more like labor pains now. "Brad, I thought you said ..."

"Sorry, Princess. That was a little white lie. I needed to get you in here so we could have some privacy."

"I don't know what you mean." Actually, I was more than afraid I knew exactly what he meant.

"I think you do. But I can spell it out for you: I want to finish what we started last time. Tell me, Princess, when did you last let your heart decide?" He actually sang that last part.

"Brad, if I let my heart decide, it wouldn't choose you."

I could hardly believe I let myself get in this situation again. But I wasn't making a similar mistake. Or heaven forbid an even worse one. "I'm not sleeping with you, if that's what you're thinking."

"You don't have a choice, Princess. But I don't know why you're acting like this, 'cause you liked it when we kissed last time. I know you did."

I shook my head. He started walking toward me slowly. I backed up, knowing I needed to keep him talking. "That kiss was just a mistake, Brad."

"I've been thinking about you ever since, waiting for this party. But I never knew you'd show up here looking so hot. I was already interested. What are you trying to do to me, Princess?"

"This was your wife's fault. She picked our costumes." I hoped the mention of his wife would help. I didn't have high hopes.

He grinned. "Remind me to thank her later." He continued his slow waltz toward me while I continued backing up.

"Brad, I don't get it. You have a beautiful wife. Why would you want to cheat?"

He sighed. "It's like this. Take steak. I like grade A prime beef, right? But I wouldn't want to eat it every night. A man needs some variety."

I guessed now he'd be referring to me as Sloppy Joes. Or maybe tacos. I glanced toward the door wondering if I could make a run for it.

"Don't think about it, Princess. 'Cause even if you made it to the door, my good buddy Steve is keeping a lookout for intruders. And he has other orders, too. To keep you from leaving." By now I'd backed up as far as I could. I was up against a wall, literally and figuratively. Brad closed the small space between us with a single step.

I stared at him. I knew Brad was a ridiculous flirt and a probable cheat, but I didn't think he was a rapist.

It was like he read my thoughts. "Come on, Jasmine. It doesn't have to be like that. I promise you'll like it."

He put his hand on my waist and was just leaning toward me when Steve's low-pitched voice could be heard from outside, humming. I could make out the tune of, "Here Comes the Sun."

Brad groaned. "Shit, it's the wife." He pointed at his bed. "Get under," he whispered urgently.

I hesitated but he grabbed my arm and tried to shove me under. I wrenched my arm away but slid under the bed. I didn't want Elise catching me here either.

Steve's voice reached us. "Hey, Elise. Great party. Are we gonna bob for apples again? Kel loved it once she got over her hang-up."

"No. Not now, Steve. I'm looking for Brad. We need him to fix more drinks."

"I can do it for you."

"No offense, Steve, but Brad is the king. No one does Sex On The Beach like him." She laughed, the sound light and flirty.

I heard the sound of the door opening. "Hey, babe. Looking for me? I heard you want some sex on the beach. Don't you ever get tired?"

"Never. You should know that."

"Steve is an excellent bartender. The ladies never complain, right Steve?"

"But, what are you doing? Why can't you do it?"

Brad sighed. "No reason, babe."

I heard footsteps going away. But I wasn't sure if the coast was clear. Someone cleared his throat. I peeked out carefully and saw Steve standing near the bed. He was motioning for me to come out. I slid out and stood up.

"They're gone." He had a smirk on his face like he was somehow enjoying all of this. That really pissed me off.

At least Brad had his reasons for what he was doing—perverted, adulterous reasons, granted—but at least it made sense in a sick way. But why was Steve doing this?

"What's in this for you?"

"What do you mean?"

"I mean, why the hell are you enabling him? Do you think it's cool to be an accomplice to rape?"

His smirk disappeared and he looked almost sorry. "Look. I don't approve of everything Brad does. But you don't want to be on his bad side."

"My God. You're just another Tonto, aren't you?"

"What?" His eyebrows came together.

"Never mind." I started to walk out. But before I could leave, Steve stopped me.

"Uh, Beth, you shouldn't go out there like that. You have stuff all over you."

"Excuse me?" I looked down at myself and saw what he meant. There were dust bunnies all over me. "I can't believe it." To my own ears, my voice sounded full of wonder. "She has dust bunnies." I hadn't intended to speak the words out loud.

As I stood there, marveling over Elise's imperfection, Steve suddenly reached out and was, apparently, going to brush off a large bunny that was perched on my right boob.

Suddenly a voice drew our attention. "Steve! What the

hell is going on here?" It was Kelly standing in the doorway, looking furious and not at all Tonto-like.

Steve's hand was still positioned in front of my breast. He quickly brought it down. "Kel. It's not what you think. I was just brushing some bunnies off her."

"Just how stupid do you think I am, Steve?" Kelly's last words broke on a sob and she ran from the room.

Steve stood there looking dazed and confused. Suddenly I felt the need to smirk. "Payback's a bitch, huh, Steve?" That woke him up and he ran after his Snow White, fear flashing in his eyes.

So I answered Snow White's question myself. Off the top of my head, I'd say, "Pretty damn stupid."

CHAPTER THIRTEEN

THE SIDEKICK

Yet another fear of mine came true. Elise actually made us bob for apples. I didn't really think she'd do that. But there was no way I was going first because if she had some prank planned, clearly the first person would get slammed. And seeing as I was Snow White, it didn't take a genius to figure who she wanted that person to be.

But then she was so pushy. And all the guys joined in, making me feel like the ultimate chicken. So, in the end, like most things in life—in this group anyway—Elise got what she wanted. I bobbed. Only there was no prank. I didn't eat a poison apple or fall into some eternal sleep. There were no worries other than a vague sense that the bobbing in its own right had been the joke. And watching me squirm.

So, I got through that horror, but there was worse to come. I walked in on Steve about to fondle Beth. I mean, what was Elise thinking giving her that sexy costume? Still, that was no excuse for Steve's behavior.

I was so mad that I said things. In fact, I feared I said things that never should have been said—stuff about friendship. Elise had looked angry, but how bad had I messed up? How much damage was done? I didn't know, but I was really scared. As if that wasn't bad enough, I'd almost messed up even more.

I'd been this close to spilling the beans to everyone. Not just about what Steve had done. But about what I saw at the last party. But then, that would've been incredibly stupid. It's not the way the game is played. If you have goods on someone, you don't spit it out in a moment of anger. No. You bide your time. Choose an opportune moment. And only then do you strike.

THE INFORMER

I'd gone over to Beth to talk to her when she first showed up at the party. It had been a gut reaction; I knew she must be uncomfortable with every guy in the room staring. But for the rest of the party I knew I needed to be careful. I'd already shown her too much attention. So, I reverted back into old Ronnie, stick-my-neck-out-for-nobody Ronnie. After all, wasn't that who I was?

I was aware of Beth coming into the room when we were in our tight circle. I could feel her presence but I ignored her along with the rest. I didn't feel bad about that. Actually, I felt nothing. Alcohol is good for that. It was shortly after Beth walked out of the room when the craziness happened.

Our circle broke the minute Beth left. We drifted about the room and since we'd all been drinking, I'm not even sure of the exact events. People walked out and in. Jokes were told and games played, but I only remember some of it. I remember Elise trying to dig the knife in by saying, "Ronnie, are you pleased with my choice? You are, after all, our reading girl." She laughed. "And Ian is such a good sport. It's not every man who would agree to be a beast among princes."

He hadn't agreed to anything. Anyway, I forced a smile and a laugh. But all that was insignificant compared to what happened next.

Kelly came barreling into the room, looking angry and worse—or better, considering your perspective—out of control. Not a good thing to be in this group. Not that I felt sympathy for her. In fact, my brain went right to work on how I could use this to my advantage. Brad came in holding some drinks and staring at Kelly.

Kelly muttered, "I can't believe the bastard would do that." Elise went over to her right away, all fake concern. Brad noticed what was happening too. He had a strange expression on his face, a combination of curiosity and something else. Maybe anger?

Elise put her hand on Kelly's arm. "What's wrong, Kelly?"

"You'll never believe what just happened. I ..."

Just then Steve came running into the room, looking eerily like his wife. "Kel, we need to talk."

"Don't you try to talk to me now. What can you possibly say?"

Steve's eyes darted around the room. "Kel, think about what you're doing. Let's go talk in private."

"Why? Why shouldn't I tell my friends? Don't friends support each other? If they can't do that, then what freaking good are they?"

The room got quiet. Too quiet. The look on Elise's face just then reminded me of the ice queen from Narnia, only scarier. And I don't scare easily. It was like suddenly she wasn't the perfect Cinderella, the—on the surface, anyway—nice and friendly woman who'd do anything for her friends, the Queen of the princesses, the one who all the cute and furry animals loved. This new Cinderella might attract some animals, but they wouldn't be the cute and furry kind.

The look on Kelly's face also changed—drastically. It was obvious that she suddenly knew she'd said too much. That she'd let her anger that stemmed from some problem with Steve get her to admit other issues out loud. Issues that should never have been said in front of all of us. And definitely not to the queen herself.

I had to work to keep the smirk off my face. Because Kelly had screwed up big time. And she knew it.

"Elise. I ... that came out wrong ... I mean ...."

Steve used the opportunity to grab his wife's arm. "Kel, let's go talk." He glanced nervously at all of us. "She's mad at me, that's all. But we'll work it out."

She allowed him to lead her out of the room.

I looked back at Elise. Her face was composed again. But the eyes were different than they'd been. Harder. Meaner. I knew that Kelly would pay for her mistake. Just how big a mortgage she'd need to cover the fee remained to be seen.

THE WANNABE

So, I walked into the party dressed in my frumpy Mulan getup, with Joe for once actually almost looking better than me, and I caught Elise's triumphant smile. She knew this was killing me. I do not do frumpy. Or tomboy.

And then, to make matters worse, Beth walked in after me. Elise asked for her coat and all the guys were like immediately chomping at the bit. And that could've been me. By all rights should have been me. So why the hell did she give that costume to Beth? Actually to Beth, who is supposed to be the lowest of the low? She's still on probation, not even a legit member, yet she gets Jasmine? Where is the justice?

But that wasn't even it. Then I see Ronnie, who got Belle, Elise herself as Cinderella, like we all knew, and Kelly as Snow White. Clearly, liked I'd feared when I'd received my choice, I'd gotten the worst. Was this some message Elise was sending me? Was she trying to say I was now in last place, usurped by newcomer Beth? And if so, why? What had I done to deserve that demotion?

I had the hardest time ever keeping the fake smile on. To pretend all was peachy. I may have indulged a bit more than usual in the Sex On The Beach, but then I needed something to get me through this. I'd use whatever I had to.

Elise came over to me at one point. "So, Gail. Happy with my choice?"

"It's great, Elise. I mean who doesn't like a strong woman like Mulan?"

"Yes. Exactly my thought. But I was a little ... worried that maybe you wouldn't feel that way. I know this costume is a bit more sedated than your usual attire."

"It's great." I smiled bigger than ever. "And Joe looks great too."

"Yes. I noticed. That costume really becomes him, somehow. I was very pleased with my choice. For both of you."

She walked away and I dug my fingernails into my hand. To avoid screaming.

Soon after came some weirdness with Kelly. I'd never seen her like that, so close to losing total control. It was a beauteous thing to behold. Because none of us, not even

Elise's number one, were secure in our place. And Kelly's fall—I didn't have to have Ronnie's smarts to know that it must be a fall—could only mean good things for me.

THE QUEEN BEE

It was the party from hell. Perhaps too appropriate given it was Halloween, or more accurately, mischief night. But there'd been much more horror than mischief. Mischief I could do, in fact I did do, often and with cold precision. And yes, I dabbled in horror to some degree I guess, although that could only be judged through the eyes of my victims.

But on this night the shoe was on the other foot. True, I'd scored some points and achieved a lot of what I wanted to achieve, but I'd taken some heavy losses too. And I wasn't used to that. Maybe I'd become too complacent. Too sure that things would always go my way.

Kelly's outburst was totally unexpected and unfortunate. Because I'd grown fond of the girl, I realized now. I'd gotten used to having her by my side, supporting me unconditionally through everything, even the most outrageous setups and pranks. But now the jig was up. Something had to change. And probably drastically. I couldn't let her get away with what she'd said. Because what kind of message would that send to the others?

I wasn't sure yet what to do about her. I'd have to think about that later. Because sadly, that was the lesser horror of the night. Now, as I lay back in the bathtub, hoping a long hot soak would help relieve my tension, my brain went back and relived that other horror all over again.

Wanting to take a break from my posse after that scene with Kelly, I went to check on Jordan and her crew. But I was surprised to find she wasn't with her friends. A quick scan of the room told me that Beth's son was also missing.

That fact brought a rush of cold fear into my heart. It couldn't be what I was thinking. The girl was smarter than that, wasn't she? She wouldn't dare go against me. Would she?

With shaky legs I climbed the stairs. It was quiet upstairs. Maybe she wasn't here after all. But I needed to check. I walked down the hall to her room. I tried the door, half-expecting it to be locked. But the doorknob turned easily in my hand. I felt relief. Because if she was in here, doing something she shouldn't be, then it would be locked.

I swung the door open and stepped inside. And was greeted by my worst fears being realized. My daughter was there. With that boy. And they were doing something all right. Something they shouldn't be. I don't even like to put a name to it. Not that I'm a prude—far from it, actually. But when your own daughter is doing this stuff, your inner prude comes out. Put it like this: my daughter was on her knees. He wasn't. And worse, he had his headphones on. Like he couldn't be bothered to remove them even when my daughter was ... doing that. For some reason that bothered me almost as much as the act itself.

I don't usually lose control. Or if I do, it's a controlled loss of temper. But I couldn't stop myself from screaming, "Jordan. What the hell is going on?" Such a stupid question. Again, totally unlike me. Because any moron could plainly see what was going on.

I'll never forget what happened next. Jordan stopped and turned calmly to me, like she knew I'd show up all along and wasn't even bothered by it. She looked me in the eye. "It's pretty obvious, isn't it, Mom?"

Rico Jr. at least had the decency to quickly pull up his pants and look embarrassed. The same could not be said for my daughter. She looked calm, cool, and not in the least bothered by the situation.

"Jordan, go downstairs right now. And get away from this boy who is so beneath you."

"Uh, Mom? I was actually beneath ..."

"Jordan, leave the room this instant or I will send all your friends home."

"Kind of an empty threat, isn't it? Since appearances are all important to you. What would you tell their parents? That your daughter got caught giving ..."

"Jordan! Do not put me to the test. I will do what I have to do. I can force your friends home for other reasons than your unacceptable behavior." Just then, I caught the boy trying to sneak out of the room. "Oh, no, Junior. You're staying here and I'm going to inform your parents of this episode."

"He shouldn't get in trouble. It was my idea."

"Jordan, I do not want to hear one more word out of your mouth." I squeezed my eyes shut for a minute. Suddenly my head ached. "You know what? Both of you get out of here. I can't stand looking at either of you."

I turned to Junior. "But know this, young man. Your parents will hear about this. And you are forbidden to ever enter my house again. We clear?"

"Yes, ma'am." The "ma'am" was another dagger in my heart. I grimaced and he walked out quickly.

At Jordan's laughter, my head snapped back toward her. "Go ahead and be all, 'I forbid you, young man.' How predictable. You're just like any other mom. So ... ordinary."

I've never been so close to hitting my own child. We stared at each other like rival prizefighters for several moments. Actually, not like that. Because we had more real hatred going on. She finally broke eye contact, turned, and left. Although I won that round, it didn't come easily or without pain.

My daughter was not afraid of me. That much had been made clear. But what bothered me even more was the anger in her eyes, that cold, hard anger. And how when I looked at her, it was like looking in a mirror.

THE TARGET

Toward the end of the night, Elise walked into the room and made a beeline for me. My gut reaction was to flee, but she was too good at zeroing in on her prey. "Beth, please come to my room for a minute. There's something I'd like to show you."

She wanted to show me something? In her room? Like some sketches? Wasn't that a guy's line? She was even less original than her Prince Charming hubby.

I hesitated but Elise grabbed my arm and steered me away from Rick, who was back by my side. I looked over my shoulder and saw Rick watching us with raised brows. I wanted to mouth "Help," but feared Elise would see. We walked together without speaking and then entered the room I'd left only several minutes ago. She closed the door and locked it. This was all so familiar. But what could Elise want? Surely not the same thing her Prince Charming hubby wanted.

"Beth. Don't look at me like that for Heaven's sake. I'm not a lesbian. Or a serial killer. Or whatever ridiculous thought is going through your head. I just needed to talk to you in private." She sounded uncharacteristically annoyed. She was usually cool and calm in the face of everything.

"Sure. That's what I figured." I tried to look and sound unruffled.

"You need to be made aware of something that just occurred." She stopped, taking a deep breath. "Your lovely son somehow convinced my daughter to perform a certain sex act on him. I'm assuming I don't have to put a name to it. You're a big girl. I'm sure you know what I mean." She paused, watching my face. I would've liked to think I kept my placid exterior, but I knew I didn't. I could feel my jaw dropping practically to the floor till I managed to pull it back into place. I wasn't capable of responding.

Elise went on, "For obvious reasons I wanted to inform you of this. I assume you'll be punishing him appropriately."

I found my voice. "Are you sure that ..."

"You think I'd lie about this?" Anger flashed across her face.

"No, it's just that I have a hard time ..."

"I saw it with my own eyes. Unfortunately, there can be no doubt." She paused and made a face that showed all too clearly what she thought of what she'd seen. "In fact, I'll give you another bit of information. He didn't bother to remove his headphones."

I didn't know what to say. I was still full of shock. But I managed to force out a few words. "Of course he'll be talked to and punished."

Elise laughed, but the sound was cold and hard. "Good luck with talking. But just so you know, he is no longer welcome in my house." She paused. "But really, Beth, maybe it's all we can expect. He is the son of a man from another race. And Hispanics undoubtedly have a different moral code. Or maybe no moral code? You would know best. But we can't expect everyone to live up to our standards. And after all, you reap what you sow."

I stared at her, still in shock over Ricky's stupidity, but now feeling a new shock from her unbelievably racist comments. So, since my son was Hispanic, he must have no morals in Elise's view. Really? What about her husband? His whiteness had clearly not kept him from his bad, immoral behavior. But to lose my temper would only play into her hands. I wouldn't make the same mistake Kelly had earlier. Although it took a great effort, I kept my voice even.

"Well. Thanks for informing me, Elise. And my husband and I will certainly take action."

"I sincerely hope that you do. And as for our relationship, I'll have to think that over. I'd hate for this to destroy our budding friendship."

Did she actually say friendship? I felt like gagging.

"I'll need some time to figure all this out. A lot has happened today."

On her last words I thought she suddenly looked tired. Tired and less invincible.

But the moment passed, and she was again the competent and capable queen bee. "Anyway. Please collect your children and go. I'm sure you understand that the very sight of him makes me ill." She paused. "Also, although this should be obvious, I'll spell it out for you. This incident between our children must never get out. If it does, I'll know who's to blame. And I will act accordingly."

I nodded in reply and left the room. It hadn't been necessary for her to tell me to leave. In my head, I was already gone.

THE INFORMER

At home I could finally take off the ridiculous ball gown and Ian could take off that beast costume. The poor guy was sweating in that thing so much that it was almost cruel and unusual punishment, beyond the embarrassment of having to wear the stupid thing in the first place. He was truly the King, a prince among men to put up with that costume when all the other men were made up to be Prince Charmings. I'd take my beast any day.

I settled into bed, thinking over the party. I knew something big had happened toward the end. Bigger even than Kelly losing her cool and saying that stuff to Elise. I heard some commotion going on upstairs; in fact, I think everyone heard. Brad tried to smooth it over saying it was just Jordan and some of her friends joking around. But I'd heard Elise scream—I knew it was her voice. So, I pretended I had to go to the bathroom. But really, I was spying.

I knew their house so well that I knew how sound carried. I knew if I stood in the same location but a floor beneath, I'd be able to overhear the conversation overhead. I'd done it before. And conveniently the bathroom was right under Jordan's room.

So I got an earful just as Elise had gotten an eyeful. It was almost funny how easy it was for me to get information. Sometimes it came without any work on my part at all and other times, like now, it involved only a small effort. But this time I'd been hugely rewarded for that minimal work. I really had something on Elise now. Although not on her, it was something Elise would clearly wish to remain unknown. But unfortunately, it also involved Beth's son. Which made the whole thing dicey.

What would I do with this new dirt? I didn't know yet. The tricky part was always what to do with it. Two choices were to wait to strike or pounce immediately. Still another was to hand it off to a third party. But now, a fourth option occurred to me. I could do nothing. Oddly, that option was the most tempting.

Because now I had something on the one person I didn't want to have anything on. I was in a dilemma—a battle really—with my own conscience. Should I do what I always do? Or should I start out in a brand-new direction? Become a new and better Ronnie? But wasn't it too late? It seemed far too late to suddenly go down a different path, even if I was now sure it was the right path.

I had a little time to decide. But eventually I'd have to choose. It would be a test, a true test, of the kind of person I wanted to be.

CHAPTER FOURTEEN

THE TARGET

"What the hell were you thinking?" I still could not come to grips with what my son did. How my own son had screwed up my life by committing an unspeakable act with the daughter of a woman who was always screwing me.

Ricky shook his head and stared at the floor, no doubt knowing that there was nothing he could say in his own defense. Nothing that would stop my anger from flowing all over him.

"I just cannot believe this. Do you know how horrible it was for me to hear that? From Elise of all people? Do you have any idea what you've done to me? How difficult you've made my life?"

Rick Sr. cleared his throat. "*Caro*, I'm not sure I follow you. She's your friend, right? So yeah, it's awkward but ..."

I snorted. "Friend. Right. Sure."

He looked at me in confusion.

I sighed with annoyance. "Never mind. Just ... talk to the boy. You must have something to say to him about this."

Rick cleared his throat again and looked uncomfortable. He hesitated.

I glared at him.

"Okay. Right. Listen Ricky. It was disrespectful to keep your headphones on during ... while she was ... I mean you should have taken off your headphones at least. I mean, you should be more involved in what's going on."

I stared at Rick.

He stared back. "What?"

"That's all you have to say?"

"Er. No. I was just getting warmed up."

"Okay. Continue then."

"Right. So. Um." He stopped, looking confused.

"Really? You can't think of anything else to say to him?" I was struggling not to shout.

"Sure, I can." But only silence followed.

"Never mind. I can see we're not on the same page. I'll have to handle this. Big surprise." I turned to Ricky, glaring at him.

Ricky groaned. "Dad, please. Can't you handle it?"

"Sorry, son. You brought this on yourself."

I took a deep breath. "I am not going to be the type of parent who's afraid to talk to their kids about sex. The ones that stick their head up their asses and pretend their kids are little angels."

Ricky sighed loudly. "Mom, I know the facts of life." He sounded whiny.

"I'm sure you do. But clearly there are plenty of other things you don't know. Like that these kinds of sexual acts should only occur between two people who love each other and have a committed relationship."

Rick nodded. "Exactly. That's what I was going to say." I managed to avoid rolling my eyes at him.

Ricky sighed again. "It was her idea, Dad."

"It was?" Rick and I echoed each other.

"Yeah." Ricky suddenly looked more hopeful.

So. Elise had lied about that. She'd made it sound like it was all Ricky. But then I realized it didn't change anything. Elise would still hate us both, maybe all the more.

Rick looked at me. "That changes …"

"Nothing. It changes nothing." I glared at Ricky. "You have a mouth. You could have said no." I sighed in annoyance. "Do you even like her?"

He shrugged. "She's pretty. But I don't really know her."

"Exactly. And should you be doing stuff like that with someone you don't even know? Someone who I might add is only in middle school?"

He shrugged again. "I guess not."

"You shouldn't. Do you think you should be toying with this girl's emotions?"

"Mom, please. She doesn't even like me."

"What do you mean?"

"She was just trying to get back at her mom."

"How do you know?"

"It was so obvious. She left the door unlocked."

I stared at him. "Why didn't you lock it?"

"I don't know. I wasn't thinking, I guess …"

I winced. "Clearly."

"Are we done yet?"

I sighed. In truth, I was as anxious to be done as he was. "For now. But your dad and I will discuss your punishment. And I promise you, it'll hurt. In fact, since you're so fond of electronic devices, we'll include some in your punishment. Along with that area of your body that was seeing all the action."

Ricky stared at me, wincing. Rick Sr. winced too, but then I saw him suppress a grin. I guess he thought I was joking. I wasn't.

THE SIDEKICK

Seeing Steve with Beth had made my world tilt unnaturally. But luckily it had been just a brief shaking. Steve explained what happened and I believed him. The trouble was that soon I knew my world would be rocking again. Only this time it wouldn't be brief. The queen must have her revenge. I knew I'd pay for my outburst. I didn't know exactly how. But the very idea that I wouldn't be her number one anymore, that she'd toss me aside like a used condom, that was the thought that kept me awake at night. I couldn't envision a world where I wasn't with her every step of the way, sharing all her joys and sorrows like they were my own.

I'm not sure how I let it get like this. How did I allow myself to become so ingrained, so much a part of her? And how can I extricate myself from her? It sounds ridiculous when put so bluntly, but how can I live without her?

I knew Steve could be a way back. I could look to him, like maybe I should have been doing all along. He could be my rock. But ... I have always craved female companionship. Support, camaraderie, and yes, love, damn it. Steve still rung my bell and all that. But the strong bond of female friendship was something else. Guys just didn't get it. They didn't understand why we need that. And why it would hurt so much to lose it.

But I wasn't going down without a fight. I had some cards to play. It was time. If my world was gonna rock, then damn it, so would everyone else's.

THE WANNABE

The day after the ghoulish Halloween party I was hanging at home. It was a lazy Saturday morning and I was just happy to be with my family, people who loved me and weren't looking to backstab me every two seconds. I didn't even mind that Nina was watching her nonpublic TV shows. I didn't mind that she was munching on her second bowl of Froot Loops, sitting around in her ratty old jeans. I didn't give a shit about that stuff. I was just happy to cuddle with my daughter; I had set my own empty cereal bowl on the table next to me.

Joe was on the computer, and I asked him to check my email. Suddenly he began sputtering. I turned and saw milk and bits of cereal shooting out of his mouth.

"You okay?" I assumed he'd just swallowed the wrong way, but although he stopped spitting and coughing, he continued to have a disturbed look on his face. He stared at the computer, saying nothing. I broke away from Nina and went to him. "What?"

He just pointed at the screen, his eyes glued to it. Then I saw. And had I been eating anything it would have gone the way Joe's food had. Because there was a YouTube-type video playing from Elise's house, from the party—from the end-of-summer fling. It was taken in Elise's bedroom. Only Elise wasn't there. Brad was. And he wasn't alone. He was with me.

Something had happened between us that day. It was nothing. At least what I remembered wasn't much. We didn't have sex. Yes, I knew things had gone too far but it wasn't any big thing. That's what I'd told myself whenever I remembered that day. But now, looking at this video, the cold hard proof staring both me—and my husband—in the face, it was hard to call it nothing.

Then I remembered Nina. Good thing she was busy with Sponge Bob and had heard nothing. I sent her upstairs anyway. No way did I want her to hear about this. Or, heaven forbid, see anything.

I didn't want to see anything myself. In fact, I reached for the off button, but Joe's hand shot out and caught my arm. He shoved it away. "It's not what you think," I tried. But even as I said the words, I knew how lame they were.

"What should I think then, Gail?" He sounded sarcastic. Bitter. Angry. Who the hell could blame him?

"It was just ... we were both drunk. I mean ... I didn't mean to ... it didn't mean anything. He's a ... freaking jerk. I ... I don't even like him."

"No. I can see that. I guess someone forced you to roll around with him on his bed. In your underwear." My horrible giggling blared from the computer speakers as Brad's hand reached out to unhook my bra. "Yeah. Clearly you hate the asshole."

"Joe, I ..."

He stood up. "I'm outta here."

"Joe. Please ... wait! I can explain."

He grabbed his keys and was out the door before I could say anything else. I yanked the computer plug from the wall and fell into his still warm chair.

I felt myself shaking. Next I was sobbing. My head spun from just how quickly my morning had turned into a horror show. Among the many painful thoughts swirling through my brain, one question finally broke through: Which one? Which one of my "friends" had screwed me this time?

THE QUEEN BEE

I woke up in a gloomy mood. Gloomy was unusual for me. After a party, I was usually into all-out gloat mode. Thinking over the details of a previous shin-dig was usually an enjoyable way to spend a free day. But after this Halloween stinker, there was little to gloat over.

There'd been bad news on several fronts. Kelly's public dissing of me occupied much of my thoughts. That was sometimes pushed out by Jordan's atrocious behavior and betrayal. Then there was the memory of Brad's eyes frequently seeking Beth's cleavage. And who did I have to blame for that last point? I admitted that costume choice was a rare failure.

When I tried to turn my thoughts to what went right, it was an effort to keep them there. I'd gotten some digs in with my costumes of choice and the apple bobbing, but my losses outweighed the gains by far. Was I losing my touch? Or was it just an off night?

Today, Sunday—the first day of the week—should have been a rebirth. A fresh start. So, I decided I would try to banish my troublesome negative thoughts. Cup of coffee in hand, I sat down at the computer. I'd check Facebook and maybe play a little with my friends. Chat online with them and bring up some old wounds or something. But first I checked my email.

Then, I saw it. I rubbed my eyes. It couldn't be. This was a trick. Something worthy of ... well, my own kinds of tricks. Yet ... it looked real. I didn't see how or for that matter why someone would fake this. No one I knew would have the guts to do this. To me. None of my posse would dare ... no, impossible. But if it was real then what exactly did that mean?

I sighed heavily and did something totally unlike me. I hunched my shoulders and buried my head in my arms. Suddenly yesterday's problems seemed like nothing.

THE WANNABE

Okay. I needed to get down to some serious thinking. Who did this to me? Who showed the whole world my little frolic with Brad? Well, it wasn't exactly the whole world— the link to the YouTube video from hell had been sent to me via email from what was clearly a pseudonym, someone called Snow Queen. When I typed in the address in the search engine I was taken to the horrible video. Still, a person would need to know the address to get there.

But then oddly, when I checked later that day, the video was gone. Snow Queen appeared to be messing with my mind. Making me wonder what her next move would be. Along with wondering who had seen the video besides my husband and me. Had Snow Queen sent it to any of my other friends? Had Elise seen it? That was the question that tormented me most.

But the most pressing question was, *Who is Snow Queen?* On a hunch I decided to check Facebook to see if there were any clues there. I discovered with a chill that I was actually friends with a person call Snow Queen, yet I didn't remember friending her. Then again, Elise stressed numbers above all else. The way the popularity game was played—online anyway—it was all about quantity, not quality. So I said yes to everybody. We all did.

But who the hell was she? I looked up her profile and

a chill went down my spine. Because the profile pic was—not surprisingly I guess—the Narnia queen. I'd always thought how odd it was how someone so beautiful could be so menacing. Now I was again struck with that thought.

With an effort, I reminded myself the Snow Queen didn't exist. She was just a figment of an author and a director's imagination, nothing more. I clicked on Snow's home page. Maybe there would be some clues as to who was using her as a cover.

Her page was—in a word—creepy, but it was of little help. There were only three pictures and they were all Narnia related, mostly the queen looking evil and threatening. I thought briefly about whether whoever did this had the copyright for these pictures, but then I looked closer and saw that it wasn't the actress from the movie. It was actually someone else, someone who looked disturbingly like her. But it was not someone I knew.

I went to her info page, still looking for clues, but all the interests were again related to that same theme. Lion hunting was listed as a favorite activity and favorite movie was a no brainer. I didn't think her favorite quote was from the movie, however. It said, "An insincere and evil friend is more to be feared than a wild beast; a wild beast may wound your body, but an evil friend will wound your mind." Wow. That was deep. And strangely unsettling.

I noticed something listed under siblings. It had Elise's name listed as a sister. She was the only family member listed. Weird.

Snow was listed as being in a relationship. I guessed the lucky man would be a fictional dude. It turned out to be someone called Butch Cavendish. That name sounded familiar, but I wasn't sure why. When I tried to go to his page only a little info came up because he wasn't a friend. There was no picture of him, just a cartoon gun. Who knew what that meant?

So, although Snow's pages were creepy, I still didn't know who she was. Or really which of my friends was using that alias, because it had to be one of them. Who else could possibly have gotten a video of what happened?

My first thought was Elise since she did look a little like the queen from Narnia. But that made no sense. It couldn't be her. Could it? Was she twisted enough to risk others seeing something that would bring the most pain to herself? I didn't think so.

I could rule out Beth, because she wasn't like that. Unless her time with us had corrupted her sooner and faster than ever before. But I didn't think she had it in her. Clearly a hidden camera was involved, which logically would point to Elise since it was her house. Or ... someone else who'd been devious enough to plant one in the queen's own house without her knowledge. And that thought led my brain right to the obvious—Ronnie. That's it. It had to be her. No one else had the nerve or ability to pull something like that off.

And that figured. Oh, how that figured. How many times had she already done this kind of shit? At least once, and maybe a hell of a lot more. Well, I might not have her smarts or her luck, but I suddenly knew I wasn't taking this lying down. Not anymore.

I would fight back. Somehow. Someway. A new day was dawning in the burbs. And with any luck they'd never be the same again.

THE TARGET

I skipped the bus stop today. I just couldn't face seeing Elise after the embarrassing events of that party. I had no clue how she would treat me now. But experience told me it couldn't possibly be good. I mean for lesser offenses—or often no offenses—she had dished out some severe "punishments." Now that she had a real reason to be pissed, who knew what she would do?

It was weird because I thought I'd seen Elise at pickup—or someone who looked just like her at any rate. She was running out with a young blonde girl who from the back looked like her daughter. The mom was wearing dark shades and a raincoat with the hood pulled up. If it was Elise, it was really weird. First, she never missed the bus stop. It was like her office, the place where she called the shots and heads rolled, so to speak. Secondly, why the spy getup? Why the apparent desire to avoid everyone? That was just not her style. No. It probably wasn't her despite the likeness.

Then even weirder, I saw Gail waiting in the cafe at pickup. I figured she'd ignore me or maybe just give a quick nod or something, but instead she walked right up to me.

"Hi, Beth."

"Hi." Oddly we'd never talked just the two of us. Now it felt weird.

"So." She paused then quickly went on, "What are you doing here?"

I gave her a look. Maybe she was really as dumb as Elise liked to imply? I started with the obvious answer, "Picking up …"

She started to roll her eyes but stopped mid-roll. "I know that. I mean why not the bus stop?"

I hesitated. Should I give some excuse? I sure didn't want to admit the real reason: Elise avoidance. So I started to mumble, "Well, um, Selena wanted to get home early because um ..."

She gave me a knowing look. "Don't worry. I didn't want to see her either." Okay. So not as dumb as Elise thought. I felt guilty for my not-so-nice thoughts. But then again, these women could do that to a girl.

But why was Gail suddenly all cozy with me?

Gail looked uncertain and uncomfortable. "Look. Can I tell you something?"

I wanted to say no. But that would sound mean and then I realized she was looking at me in an almost pleading way. I sighed. "Okay."

But I couldn't believe the stuff she told me. It made my head spin. And why confide in me of all people? But then it hit me. I was her last hope.

CHAPTER FIFTEEN

THE SIDEKICK

The thing is I didn't need her. That thought was both liberating and empowering. After all, even the queen always had to have a backup, a helper. But not me. I would go it alone. I knew I had the power to screw her. Big time. And that was just too tempting to pass up.

Because she'd made a fatal error, one that never in a million years would I have expected of her. She allowed herself to get too close. Maybe she thought she could pull it off, being both the good guy and the bad guy simultaneously. But she should know by now how impossible that was. And if she didn't before, she did now. After today.

I replayed the scene with her in my head. How I'd knocked on her door. How she'd opened it with a momentary surprised look that quickly gave way to her usual game face. "Hey, Kelly." Her voice was smooth. I planned to make that change.

"Hey. Got a second?"

The briefest annoyance crossed her face, but she pushed open the door. We walked to her kitchen. "Coffee?" she tossed over her shoulder.

"Never touch the stuff. Didn't you know I prefer something harder?" Showed how good friends we were. She didn't even know that about me. I wondered suddenly if Elise knew.

She looked over her shoulder with slightly raised brows. "You want whiskey or something?"

"Don't tempt me." I felt lighthearted enough to banter with her. I was going to enjoy this.

She grabbed her coffee mug and we sat down. We were both silent. Her fingers drummed lightly on the table, the only sign she was impatient. "So," she finally said.

I knew I was getting to her. But she shouldn't be impatient. Not for this. She should enjoy her last few moments of blissful ignorance.

"So." I smiled a lazy grin and watched her face.

She got a weird look on her face, like maybe she doubted my sanity. "Look, Kelly, I've got some stuff I should be doing so if you could ..."

"Sure. I won't waste any more of your time." I started to rise.

"That's not what I mean. But I thought you had something to say to me."

I sat back down. "I do." I was tempted to add, *All in good time, my pretty*. But then she'd be right about the sanity thing. "Okay. Here's the thing, Ronnie. I'm making you choose."

She raised her eyebrows again, yet managing to keep her mask-like face. "Choose?"

"That's right. Between two things you love. Or like, at least."

"What two things would those be, Kel?" I hated her then. For that smug look on her face, for the look that said clearly, you can't touch me, you got nothing.

So I kept my eyes firmly on hers when I spoke because I wanted to see it—the exact moment the smugness left.

"You remember when Beth came back to the group? After you screwed her with your fashion recommendation?" I paused a beat and saw anger flash in her eyes. That was a good start, but I was just getting warmed up. "Well, I'm guessing you groveled to get her to come back. And no doubt lied about your part. But here's some news for you: I'm the one who got her back. Not you."

"Sure you did." She was going for a sarcastic tone, but she didn't quite make it.

"I did, Veronica." I paused, watching her face. She hated to be called by her full name. Sure enough, I saw that anger again. I was deadly calm. "You see, I sent a letter, explaining that I knew what happened at the summer fling. And so would everyone else, unless she came back to our little group. Naturally, the letter was anonymous." I paused and saw uncertainty on her face for the first time. "You might want to consider anonymity, Ronnie. It comes in handy sometimes."

"What exactly happened at the summer fling?" Her words were guarded but I could hear the annoyance in her voice. She hated that I knew something she didn't.

"Here. Since you asked." I tossed her the proof. Pictures of Brad and Beth together. That hidden camera of mine hit some serious pay dirt that day—two for the price of one. There were some benefits of being a cop's wife. Like playing with his toys—and I'm not just talking handcuffs.

Her eyes widened in surprise as she looked at the pictures. But she quickly pulled back into her poker face. Neither of us said anything for a full minute. Finally, she said, "And you're showing me these because ..."

"Right. Now for the choice I spoke of. You can either give these to Beth's husband, along with a letter describing their ongoing affair, or I'll have to tell Beth the truth about your little prank. The choice is yours. If you pick doing what you love—tattling on your friend—then you can give the pictures. If you choose protecting your newfound friend then unfortunately I'll have to show her exactly what kind of friend you are."

"Some choice," Ronnie muttered under her breath. "What makes you think she'll believe you? About me?" But I could hear it in her voice. The uncertainty. And I knew she was trying to convince herself as much as me.

"I think we both know she will. So, choose wisely. You have until midnight tonight."

"Do you have to be so ridiculously dramatic?" She sighed, but then laughed, the sound hollow. "That's not even a full day."

"Yeah, well, deal with it. You're the clever one, right?" I could hear the sneer in my own words. "This choice should be easy for you."

But what she didn't know was that it didn't matter. I held all the cards. And I was playing them. Every last one.

THE INFORMER

Some choice I thought again. But this time for a different reason. There was really no choice. I saw that clearly enough.

Interesting though, how Kelly thought she was all that. How she thought she finally got me and where it hurts too. But I had to hand it to her. I didn't think she had it in her. I was almost proud of her. Or, at least, I could see where the old me might have been.

But she wasn't as good as she thought. Because I knew

what she would do. It takes a snake to know a snake, I guess. It didn't take a genius to see that she was going to tell Beth about me no matter what I did. And I knew those photos would wind up hurting Beth one way or another. Maybe it would be better coming from me? Maybe I could soften the blow or prepare her somehow. But would she believe I wasn't responsible? For the pictures at least?

No, there really wasn't a choice. It was more a decision, how to handle this situation that she had thrown at me. And in that respect Tonto had provided a worthy puzzle indeed.

THE TARGET

I sat down to some TV since the kids were in bed or, in Ricky's case, upstairs in his room. Rick was working late, which was an oddity too. Normally he was an 8-to-6-er, but he'd left me a brief, almost cryptic email saying he'd be late tonight.

I was just getting into a movie when I heard the door. "You're home late," I called over to him. When I got no answer, I looked over my shoulder.

He was standing by the door, watching me with a dark, almost piercing look.

"What?" I paused, thinking something must have happened at work. I hoped he wasn't fired. But we'd deal with whatever it was, somehow. Come to think of it, maybe firing wouldn't be so bad—it could be a chance to start fresh somewhere else. Somewhere where nice people lived. That thought cheered me. "Did something happen at work?"

His face stayed dark and unreadable. He was quiet for so long I wondered whether he'd heard me. But finally he shook his head slightly and walked toward me. I noticed a package in his hands. He threw it in my lap.

"What is this?"

"Open it." They were the first words he'd spoken. From just those two words I suddenly realized he was angry.

What could be in there that would have that effect on him? Having no choice, I opened it with slightly shaking hands. I reached in and felt photos. I pulled them out and sucked in my breath. They were pictures of me. With Brad. Pictures of us kissing, and worse than kissing, because in one shot his hand was actually on my breast. And unbelievably there was even one from the Halloween party. In that shot it looked like we were about to kiss, although most of my face wasn't visible.

"How ... I don't ... where did you get these?"

"Where? Is that all you care about? How I got them?" I could sense his fragile hold on his temper, and the effort it was costing him not to lose it.

"No. I ... no. But I ... just ..."

"Were you ever gonna tell me?"

"Tell you?" I was stalling because my brain felt frozen. Like it couldn't process what was happening.

"Yeah, tell me, damn it. Were you going to tell me that you're having sex with that ... freaking Charming guy? Or were you just gonna keep it secret?"

Rick calling him Charming distracted me for a minute. It was funny he chose now in the middle of a marital crisis to call Brad that. But soon, the rest of Rick's words hit me.

"Sex? What are you talking about?" I paused, getting

angry at his accusation. "I never had sexual relations with that man!" The second the words were out I realized I sounded just like Bill Clinton. Even in the middle of the worst problem of our marriage, that made me want to laugh. It may have been to keep from crying, but unfortunately Rick noticed the turn my lips wanted to take.

"Glad you think this is so funny, *Caro*." He drew the last word out angrily and sarcastically. Clearly I was no longer his Caro. "There was a letter with the pictures. It said you've been having an affair with him for the last two months."

"What? That is such a lie. I never did anything ..."

"Clearly, that's a lie, Beth. You did something. Look at the pictures if you need to refresh your memory."

"We never had sex. I swear. He just kissed me once. That's all."

He shoved the picture in front of me, the one where Brad's hand was in such an incriminating place. I let out an impatient breath. "Okay. He touched me one time. But ..."

"Yeah, and what else happened just one time? And these pictures are from two different times." But before I could answer he went on, "Forget it. I can't deal with this shit now." He turned, heading for the door.

"Wait, Rick! Where are you going?" I ran after him.

The door slammed in my face. It was the only answer I got.

THE QUEEN BEE

So, the thing that I saw on my computer was a video. Of Brad. With someone, some mystery woman. Her face had been blotted out and from what little of the woman I could see, it was impossible to tell who it was. I could hear giggling, but whose voice it belonged to was also impossible to figure. And believe me I spent enough time pouring over the damn thing without coming any closer to answering the question of who it was. As for where, it kind of looked like my own bedroom, but I couldn't even be sure of that due to the poor lighting or some other trick of the cameraman. And that begged the how issue. How had this been done? And by whom?

As for when it happened, the clip included a date. Checking the calendar, I saw it was the day of the summer fling. Which meant that if it was taken from my bedroom, then the mystery woman must be one of my friends. Brad and I had been home all day, and the only other women there were members of my clan. I remembered that day, how I'd been suspicious of Brad and could have searched the room but didn't. It appeared someone, no doubt in that very same group, was showing me what I missed.

Watching that offending video, I remembered how detached I felt. Like I was far removed, lying on some plane where nothing could touch me. I just felt ... frozen. No emotion could penetrate through all the layers of ice to reach my heart.

At first anyway. But then a wave of something came. Only it wasn't jealousy. It wasn't anger. It was fear. Cold hard fear that I was losing my hold—had in fact already lost it—on my very own flock. I saw then that my group had been my rock. I saw just how much I needed to have an entourage. Without one, I felt naked. Alone. Scared. Those were not emotions I knew how to handle.

Two of my own people had done this to me. And that meant pure and simple that I was not the invincible leader I thought I was. One person had first disgraced and disrespected me and then presumably a different person had driven the knife in my back by showing me what the first had done. If the cheater feared me the way she should have, then this should not have happened. And if the tattletale feared me then she would never have told.

With this video, gone was my safe place where nothing could touch me. Gone was my complacency in this circle of friends. Gone too, might be my husband.

But oddly, that last thought bothered me the least. I mean, hadn't I known all along? Hadn't I guessed what Brad was capable of? In fact, wasn't this video tame compared to what I suspected he'd already done? This was child's play. Except for the fact it was with a friend. That was the part that burned.

Along with what I myself had done. I'd turned a blind eye to his wandering eyes, and hands and lips and ... well, all his wandering parts. I'd done what too many women before me have done. I put up with his adulterous ways. Me. Someone as strong and capable and beautiful as me. I put up with his shit. And then to have that shoved in my face by a "friend." Maybe that was the hardest thing of all.

What to do now? I hardly knew. But, as I sat with my head in my hands, I slowly came to realize this was not me. As if seeing myself from someplace above, I knew I would not play the poor pathetic fool. I saw with sudden clarity the only thing I could do. Get revenge. It was all I knew. All I was equipped for.

And maybe then I could salvage things. Maybe it wasn't too late.

After all, I was good at pretense. I could pretend all was fine. Hadn't I been doing that to some extent anyway? I'd simply keep up the façade. And in so doing, I would prove I was above all this. Better than them, like I always knew I was.

But I had to figure out who the two traitors were. As to the cheater, although in truth it could have been any of them, I guessed Gail. She was always asking about him and had the raging hormone problem.

As to who shoved this crap on me, it had to be Ronnie. Who else? Gail didn't have the brains. Beth didn't have the guts. And Kelly? That was impossible. The girl was incapable of thinking for herself or taking the initiative.

But, although it had to be Ronnie, I didn't understand why she was screwing me like this. Maybe just to prove she could? To finally be bold enough? But regardless of her reasons, I knew that this was the worst offense, worse than Beth and her son, worse than Kelly's outburst. So, Ronnie would be made to pay. Gail too. Oh, hell. Maybe they all would pay.

THE WANNABE

Well, somehow it happened. We were all back at the bus stop on a cold, wet November day. I was reminded of the old Guns N' Roses song, "Cold November Rain." The song was so hauntingly beautiful. But suddenly, I remembered the video. And how it ended in a funeral. Why did that seem eerily appropriate? But whose funeral would it be? I just prayed it wouldn't be mine.

But enough with the morbid thoughts. I had to keep my mind in the game. Because I knew now more than ever before that's all this was. A game. And finally, I was learning how to play.

I never thought I'd have the guts to show my face here at her majesty's headquarters—not after that video surfaced. Especially since I still had no idea if she'd seen it or not. Her behavior so far had given me no clue. I sort of guessed she hadn't seen it because even someone with her abilities could hardly keep some anger from showing. But that was just a guess; I really wasn't sure. And that was a scary state to be in. Knowing her wrath was coming down was almost better. At least you could be somewhat prepared when it hit.

But it's weird how a person can find inner resolve they never knew they had. It's also weird how a friend can turn up out of nowhere. Yet, I wasn't considering anyone a friend. Not really. Not ever again. But I could use people to help me. People who for their own reasons happened to be in a similar state.

I noticed Elise smirking at me, so I pulled myself back to the conversation at hand.

"So, Gail, I hope all's well with you. We've missed having you around." She laughed in a careless, yet calculated fashion. "After all, without our resident fashion diva, the rest of us barely know how to dress ourselves."

She was complimenting me? At one time a statement like that would have put a smile on my face for a week straight. Now, it turned my stomach. Just play the damn game I reminded myself.

I smiled, hoping it didn't look as weak as it felt. "Thanks, Elise. You don't know what that means to me." I smiled a little more genuinely as I realized the double meaning of my words. I was getting this yet.

She smiled back and for just a moment I thought I saw something else in her eyes. Anger. Hatred. But it melted away before I could be sure whether or not I'd just been projecting my own fears into her face.

Elise cleared her throat, an indication of some announcement coming from her lips. "Well, I don't know about the rest of you, but I need something to look forward to. Some event. Christmas is still too far away, and November is such a drab month. So, what do you ladies think about a party?" She glanced at all of us in turn.

We all nodded and said stuff in the affirmative, but it seemed to lack something. Before all the craziness, it seemed like there would have been more kissing up. Then I realized that Kelly was strangely contained. Normally she'd be all over any of Elise's ideas. True, she was nodding and saying the right stuff, yet not like before. Not with the same gusto.

Suddenly Kelly noticed me looking at her. She perked up visibly. "Elise, as usual you've said the perfect thing. Yes, let's have a party." Did I imagine that challenging look she shot me?

Elise nodded her thanks to Kelly. "But not just any party. A ball."

"A ball?" Ronnie asked, with a twinge of something. Maybe sarcasm? Annoyance? Who knew? Who cared what the wicked witch was thinking? She'd once called herself that as a kind of joke. Who knew then how true it was?

"Yes. A ball. Ronnie, I assume you know what they are.

Or has it been so long you don't remember?" She paused, then added, "Although the balls you've seen aren't quite up to my standards."

There was a weird silence. Because as evil as we all knew Elise was, she didn't usually do her dirty work so openly.

Ronnie stared back, a smile playing at the corners of her mouth. I think she liked it that Elise was starting to unravel. "I remember. I think we all do. In fact, I hear some of us have an intimate acquaintance with the type of balls you handle."

I could feel my face turning red with anger and embarrassment—I hardly knew which was stronger. Ronnie had some nerve to bring out a veiled, or not so veiled, insinuation of what Brad and I had done. I had to fight to keep my chin up and a fake smile planted on my face. My eyes darted around nervously before they met Beth's and I saw similar emotions staring back at me. Somehow knowing I had found a weird sister in arms, I suddenly felt a little stronger.

In fact, after a few seconds, I could even bring my eyes to meet Elise and Ronnie's. And what I saw was an unusual sight. It was like they were having a staring contest, both too stubborn to give in. And that silence wasn't going anywhere; it only grew more powerful and awkward with the passing seconds.

Suddenly something made me look over at Kelly. And what I saw was shocking. For just a second before she caught me looking at her, I saw eager anticipation. She appeared to be enjoying Elise's public dissing. But how could that be? By rights, she should have been well into total suck-up mode after her words to Elise at the

Halloween party. Yet, here she was, liking this situation.

But then I realized it could have been simply that Ronnie—who'd always been Elise's number one go-to person—was practically getting into an open fight with Elise. Kelly might only have been enjoying Ronnie's probable demotion. The more I thought about it, the more that seemed likely. Sidekick girl lived for pleasing Elise and seeing her pleased, so it was impossible for her to find any happiness in Elise's misfortune.

Finally, it was Beth who broke the heavy silence. "Here's the bus." A lame statement, yet effective. Suddenly we went all parental—last-minute backpack checking, goodbye kissing, and waving at the departing bus like the good parents we so weren't.

We said short goodbyes and walked to our cars. I breathed a sigh of relief. Game over.

Or more like, round over. Because unfortunately there was still much more game to be played.

CHAPTER SIXTEEN

THE TARGET

So my life was going down the toilet. Rick had left after seeing those pictures. He came back but was sleeping on the sofa and avoiding me by coming home ridiculously late and leaving wicked early. I guessed he needed time, which was okay because I felt like I needed it too.

Besides my husband troubles, I had "friendship" troubles. Right on the heels of seeing those horrible photos I'd gotten more news.

Ronnie had come to see me. And told me the truth about the bathing suit blow-up. Although I guess deep down I'd always suspected, or even knew, she was behind that, another part of me believed her apology to me. Another part of me allowed myself to be friendly with her because I chose to believe she was innocent of deliberately trying to hurt me. But now, I was forced to confront the ugly truth, and so the fragile façade I'd built came crashing down.

As painful as this was, I supposed it was slightly better than keeping up the lie. But I wondered, why come clean now? That is, until Kelly paid me a visit later the same day. Basically to tell me what Ronnie already had. When I made it clear that I already knew, and how, Kel kindly explained. "Yeah, well, Veronica had to tell you. Or she knew I would. See, I made her do it. She never would have. She would have gone on deceiving you. Because that's what she does. And there's no one better at it." She paused. "But I guess you know that now."

"What about your motives, Kel? Why are you doing this?"

"I just thought you deserved to know the truth."

My mind was spinning. These women were just so out of my league, in more ways than I could count. "Yeah, right. Clearly, honesty and integrity are a big part of who you are. Not just you. All of you."

She smirked. "I wouldn't be so high and mighty if I were you. You're hardly a saint."

"I never said I was." Her words and her look seemed to be implying something. But I couldn't think and I just wanted her gone. "Well, if that's all you came for then ..."

"Yeah. I'm gone." She got to the door but then suddenly turned. "But if you need a friend, a true friend, just remember I'll always be here for you."

I stared at her, not sure I heard her right. Her face gave nothing away. But it was clearly a joke. It had to be.

"Thanks, Kel. That means so much coming from you. But I'm sure you'll understand when I say that even if I was hanging on to a cliff and the only way up was if I let go of my tenuous hold and take your hand, I'd refuse your offer. And take my chances with the cliff."

She shrugged. "Suit yourself." But I thought I detected some emotion other than indifference.

"Don't take it personally. I feel the same about all of you."

She turned to leave. But I could have sworn I heard her answer, "What a coincidence."

THE QUEEN BEE

I'd called it a ball for two reasons. One, I gave in and used a tired double entendre to insult. But for other reasons, I simply felt like doing a fancy shindig. I needed cheering up and swanky clothing, decorations, and loads of wine. All of that might just do the trick. Or at least dull the pain.

But at this so-called ball I would put my plan into action. I'd reserved a hotel ballroom—a small one—along with a few rooms. The rooms were necessary ingredients in my plan that I was now unveiling at the bus stop headquarters. I felt something like the old excitement of putting a plan in motion. But this time that feeling was small compared to the other main emotion I'd been full of lately—anger. I just hoped that anger wouldn't blind me to the point that I'd mess up, because I had no backup now. It was all on me. But was I not the queen? Surely I could handle this. Blindfolded, hands tied behind my back.

Arriving at the bus stop and issuing a general greeting, I then asked, "So, ladies, are we ready for the ball tonight?"

My fallen-from-grace choir chimed in with appropriate responses. I continued, "Well, I have a little added surprise for you."

I checked everyone's face in turn, but instead of surprise or even fear, I saw only weary acceptance. Like yeah, what else is new? Another surprise, one that will probably mean bad things for us. True, but why not more fear? Or anger even?

I pressed on anyway. "I'm guessing you ladies all get … from time to time anyway, it happens to all of us I'm sure … a little bored. With your husbands." I laughed and hoped it sounded more sincere than I felt. "I mean, it even happens to me, and look at the beefcake I've got in my bed."

Ronnie looked at me and raised her brows. "Beefcake is surely in the eye of the diner."

I decided to rise above her little dig, if that's what it was. "Anyway, this is my plan to alleviate our sexual boredom: we're going to do a husband swap."

Now, at least the weary acceptance was gone and finally there was some shock registering. Kelly cleared her throat. "Switch husbands?" Her tone implied, "I couldn't possibly have heard you right."

"Yes, that's correct. Just for one night. And relax. This is my idea, after all, so whichever lucky woman gets Brad, she has my blessing." Yeah. Like hell.

Ronnie spoke up again. "Elise, this is an interesting idea but surely even you realize that it's just ... wrong."

"Wrong?" I shook my head and looked innocently at her. "I mean each couple can choose how far to go. You don't have to have sex if you don't want to. But if you want to then go for it. After all, when would you get an opportunity for anything like this ever again? A chance to safely live out a sexual fantasy with no strings and no worries. Actually, this kind of thing is fairly popular in certain sets. I think there's even a name for it."

"Immorality?" Ronnie smirked.

"It used to be called 'swinging.' Now I think it's called the Lifestyle or something. But Ronnie, surely a little immorality isn't beneath you. After all, we all know what you're capable of."

I smiled and we both knew it was a double-sided smile.

I wondered what my number one fan would have to say about this. I looked at Kelly. She looked back at me and shrugged. "You know me, Elise. I'll go along with whatever you want." But there was an odd tone in her voice. I wasn't sure what to make of it.

Gail picked at her fingernails. "But for something this, uh, drastic, shouldn't we get more time to think it over?"

"Who needs time? You either want to do it or you don't. Besides the ball is tonight and the rooms are already reserved. But you can let me know tonight. If that helps."

"So, we can opt out?" That was Gail, still picking.

"Of course. I can't force you to do this, can I?" I laughed and watched their faces. Obviously I'd managed to force them to do lots of stuff in the past. Just never quite this outrageous.

"How are you planning to pair people up? Pick names out of a hat?" Ronnie was barely holding back a smirk.

"It's more sophisticated than that. I have a computer program. Each person will enter a name of their desired mate—but just so you know, the computer will spit it back if you try to enter your husband's name. It's an impressive program actually. Completely anonymous, so don't worry about my knowing or, for that matter, anyone knowing who you picked. It will make the pairings based on what we enter."

Ronnie still had the annoying almost-smirk going on. "I assume you realize there's a number problem with your idea. Or does the computer program somehow allow for that?"

I nodded slightly at her. She would think of that. "You mean because we are an odd number." I shot a glance at Beth. After all, she was the reason we were odd, in more ways than one. "Yes, because of that problem, I have to include another couple." I paused dramatically, then looked slyly at Beth. "But I assume there will be no objections."

"Aren't you going to tell us who it is?" Gail asked.

"You'll find out tonight."

Beth spoke up. "But ... what if the husbands refuse?"

"Interesting question. Yet, if you believe the rap on most guys, who among them wouldn't jump at this chance to er, ... well ... jump someone else for a change? But then, I suppose not all guys are like that." I thought of Brad. He was definitely like that. I hurried on, "But if any of your husbands need convincing, that shouldn't be a problem. I mean we all know who the true power broker in any marriage is. If you ladies want this, then I'm sure you know how to make it happen."

I didn't really want them to want it. This idea was a means to an end. I wanted to see, number one, how far I could push them. How far would they go in an attempt to get back into my good graces? I was showing little miss tattletale that I could still lead. And lead boldly. I had little to lose at this stage of the game. So why not go out with a bang?

Secondly, I hoped this little game would provide the clues I needed to determine beyond a doubt which of my friends was screwing around with my husband.

THE SIDEKICK

Okay, has Elise bought her place in the funny farm? I mean, what was the woman thinking?

This whole situation is so not what I thought would happen. I assumed after my outburst she'd shun me. Or punish me in some major way. And that's why I had to strike first. But she seemed unconcerned. Or, was it just an act? She was certainly capable of that.

Confused with her response, I'd tried to be the same old diehard Kelly. Her number one supporter. But it took work keeping up the pretense.

I'd appeared to go along with her crazy husband-swap thing, because one, it was no doubt a trap—probably not for me but who knew for sure—and two, I knew she expected me to go along. That's what sidekicks do.

Weirdly there was a part of me that felt guilty over what I'd done to her. Sometimes I even wondered if I'd made a mistake. Maybe she hadn't been planning to slam me for what I'd said at the Halloween party. Maybe there was a part of our friendship that was genuine. Maybe, just maybe, we had something that could withstand a few poorly chosen words.

But then another part of me, the part that knew her best, said she was only acting like this because of what I'd done. And if I hadn't done it, she'd be shunning me big time, and worse, planning to stab me in the back. Most likely my part had forced her into her current position. That thought both thrilled and terrified me.

So now I could afford to play by her rules. I could go along with this newest game. Because I suspected I wasn't her main prey. In fact, I may have become a predator.

THE TARGET

"You want me to do what?" Rick's jaw dropped to the floor and his eyes were wide. He shook his head. "I must have heard you wrong. It sounded like you said you want me to sleep with one of your friends."

"You heard me right." Rick and I had sort of worked things out. We were talking again, and he was sleeping in our bed, not the sofa. I'd managed to convince him that the stuff with Brad wasn't as bad as he thought. All I was really guilty of was letting him kiss me and Rick had forgiven me for that.

"Uh, Beth? That's really ... ah ..."

"Weird?"

"Sick." He stared at me with his brows drawn together. "And I mean it in the old-school way, not Ricky's way."

Elise's words had made me wonder: Which type of husband was Rick? She'd made it sound like most guys would love this chance. I didn't really think that was Rick, but I couldn't help testing him. Especially because of what happened with Brad, maybe he'd want to get me back, so to speak. "So, you don't want to do it then?"

"What I don't get is why you want me to."

"It's something Elise wants to do. She said most guys would jump at this chance."

"Maybe. But not this guy."

I had my answer. I ran to him and hugged him tight.

"*Caro*, are you feeling okay? You're acting weird."

"I'm good." I was, after hearing those words from him.

"But are you serious? Do these friends of yours really expect me to do that?"

"It's not just you. I have to sleep with one of the guys."

"What?" His jaw dropped again. When he could speak, he said, "That's not happening."

"You're not okay with that, then?"

He looked at me like I had just sprouted horns. "No,

I'm not okay with that. I don't know many husbands that would be." He narrowed his eyes. "You would really do that? Maybe you do like freaking Charming, after all." He looked angry.

I struggled to keep a straight face and I shrugged. "Not him. But ... I kind of have a thing for Ian."

"Ian? But he's so chubby and ..." He dropped off, finally noticing that I was struggling not to laugh. "Ha. Very funny." He ran his hand through his hair. "But this is not funny, Beth. And I'm having a hard time understanding why you think it is."

"I don't think it's funny. I'm laughing because I see a way out. Finally. I don't care anymore what she does or says. I'm done. Truly done this time."

"I don't follow you."

I knew he wouldn't. "I'll explain." So, I did. Because I had a plan. For once. And it was worthy of anything her majesty could dish out.

THE INFORMER

Elise's counterpunch was interesting. It didn't score many points for subtlety or morality for that matter, but it was effective for her goal. I could see clearly enough what she was trying to do. I'd seen the video that an anonymous person sent me. I was pretty sure we'd all seen it and that accounted for the new weirdness in the group. I had my suspicions who was behind it, and more easily, who'd been caught with Brad.

This was Elise's answer to that video. She wanted to show she didn't care if Brad cheated, because she was going to cheat too. That was no doubt an act because for all of Elise's coldness and calculation, I felt pretty sure she actually loved the guy. Could that fact be her downfall? Trusting in a guy that should never be trusted?

She wasn't dumb; she must know Brad's ways. Yet she'd turned the other cheek, so to speak. And then to have that pointed out to her, likely by one of us—that must have been a huge blow to her ego. The blow that really hurt.

But those thoughts raised unanswered questions. I didn't know what Elise knew exactly. Had she also seen the photos of Brad and Beth? Did she know Tonto was responsible? Or did she suspect someone else? Namely, me.

Of course. It was so obvious. That was the downside of being known as the smart one. She assumed I was the culprit, totally underestimating those around her. Especially the one right under her nose—or should I say her thumb. Only Tonto wasn't under her thumb anymore. Elise just assumed she was.

Yes, she definitely thought I had done this to her. That would explain her unusually unveiled insult. Not only was she angry but she was showing that anger. And that never happened. She was becoming unglued. But surprisingly, I was enjoying the ungluing.

And the irony. Because here she was, mad at me, yet what had I done? Nothing. I wasn't the one who got those pictures of her husband fooling around. I hadn't fooled around with him. In fact, I was one of the few that hadn't done anything with Brad. Yet I was the one she hated most. Maybe it was fitting. After all, maybe there was some justice in the world. Was I finally getting my much overdue payback for all my sins?

CHAPTER SEVENTEEN

THE WANNABE

"Hey, Elise." I walked through the glamorous outer entrance way and into the small yet elegant ballroom. My fake smile was firmly planted and my voice calm—hopefully, anyway.

"Gail. So glad you finally joined us." Yup. I was last. But for once I didn't care. Screw her. Hopefully, this was the last time I'd have to listen to a comment about my lateness.

I sat down at a table with the other women. The men were arranged around another table, closer to the bar. All already had drinks in front of them. Their expressions ranged from weary, to anxious, to in Brad's case bored, but it seemed like a fake boredom.

Elise stood up. "Well, now that we're all finally here, we can begin." I glanced around but there was no extra couple. What was up with that? Then I saw Elise zeroing in on me. "Since everyone's had time to think, it's decision time. So. Who's in and who's out?"

Her hawk eyes were on me and waiting, as if I really had a choice. "We're in." I glanced over at Joe, who'd agreed pretty easily to this. We'd talked about how we weren't going to do anything with our "partner." But part of me wondered if he was planning to go through with it anyway, just to get even with me for what I'd done to him.

Elise went around the female table and everyone said yes. Elise nodded approvingly, ignoring the men. "Good, that's settled. And like I promised, we have an addition to the festivities. So, without further ado, here is the mystery couple." She sounded like a bad game show host. All eyes went to the entrance. And, on cue, in walked a middle-age guy and his middle-age wife. The guy was large in a used-to-be-a-football-player way but was now just plain fat. He still carried himself like he was all that and a bag of supersized chips. He wasn't.

His wife was more attractive than him, but not by much. And she didn't look happy. Not at all. The ex-football guy, on the other hand, looked mighty pleased with the situation, leering at all the women. He gave me the creeps. I wondered who in their right mind would pick him.

Elise put her arm in his. "So, everyone, I'd like you to meet Brian and Sondra Peters. Brian, I know you're acquainted with some of us." Elise eyed Beth briefly and I saw Beth's face turn white. Brian zeroed in on Beth, now the main target of his leering. He was practically foaming at the mouth.

Rick looked disgusted and got half out of his seat, like he was going to go to Beth to protect her. But when he realized I was watching him, he sat down and forced an awkward smile.

Elise cleared her throat. "This is the plan. We're going to enter our choices now and then find out the results. That will be followed by dinner and dancing. Oh, and I've taken the liberty of inviting a few other guests who will be arriving shortly. But the um ... extracurricular activities won't happen till the new arrivals leave." She paused. "So, let's begin." She rubbed her hands together. Now she was practically foaming at the mouth.

Lucky me, I got to go first. I walked to a small table in

the corner with a laptop. I entered my planned choice—Rick—making sure no one was watching and went back to my seat. Everyone followed suit. A tense five minutes followed while some random guy—a techie that Elise knew somehow—fiddled with the computer and then printed out little cards with a name on it. He left and Elise explained that he didn't know what was going on so we shouldn't worry about him blabbing to anyone.

She handed out our chosen partners on a slip of paper. I glanced down, but mine didn't say Rick. It said Ian. Impossible. Or ... on second thought, very possible. Elise already made our choices for us, which I should have known. I snuck a peek at Elise, and she just grinned like the Cheshire cat. I wished she would swallow a canary. A poisoned one.

THE INFORMER

I'm pretty sure none of us believed she meant what she said. Clearly the results would be her doing and whatever we put in would be monitored by her. So if she was trying to figure out who was screwing her husband I didn't see how this could work. Not if we all knew that and planned accordingly. I mean, did she think that Brad's mistress would actually enter Brad's name in her computer? Even if she promised anonymity? I don't think any of us were that gullible. Not even Gail. Or, maybe she was looking for other clues, subtler ones. Like whose cheeks looked the reddest or who was sneaking stolen glances at her beloved—that kind of thing. But what would that stuff really tell her? She still wouldn't know for sure.

Irrespective of her intentions, I played my part. I entered my choice, then waited to see whom she picked for me. Kept my poker face when I saw that I was with Steve. That was weird. But then I had no idea what to expect.

Anyway, it mattered little in the overall scheme of things whom I got paired with. My mind was on how the evening would shake down. I guess it was fitting that I was paired with a cop, since I was already using their lingo.

THE SIDEKICK

Well. I got Joe. Which was not who I picked. Big surprise. I guessed by giving me Joe, one of the least attractive men, this was yet another of her tricks, another way of screwing me. But what she didn't know was that I didn't care anymore. I had my own tricks now. And it didn't matter who she paired me with. It didn't matter what she said or thought about me anymore. I was done with her. At least, I kept trying to tell myself that.

THE TARGET

As soon as I saw Brian Sr., I knew what Elise was planning. And I knew that things had changed very little for me. I'd begun this group as a target and I'd leave it as a target. There was no moving up the ladder for me. It never happened. It never would have happened. This latest torture showed me that plainly enough. But then, I'd already figured that out.

I could tell by the creepy leer Brian was giving me that he intended to see this thing through. Thanks to my stupid words to his son, he even had reason to think I'd want it. It would make my resisting him that much harder. And the queen knew all of this and had planned accordingly.

Well, I had a plan now too. For once. Was it drastic? Extreme? Yes and yes. But sadly, this is what things had come to. At least she would finally learn something. Maybe. I had my doubts whether it was possible for Elise to learn anything. At least the lesson I wanted to teach. But either way the plan was moving forward. And things wouldn't be the same ever again.

THE QUEEN BEE

I twirled around the room going over the list in my head. Fancy dress? Check. Beautiful ballroom? Check. Flowers, gourmet food, and fun and games to follow? Check, check, and double check. But I was missing something. What was I forgetting?

Oh, right. Prince charming. I looked up at the guy spinning me around. Oh, what the hell? Check. True, Brad wasn't perfect but then who was? At least he was the best-looking man here. In his black tux, he was a spectacular specimen of manly grace and beauty. I could, for the moment anyway, forget what I knew and what I had seen. And pretend we really were living the happily ever after I deserved.

"You actually want me to sleep with that ... woman?" Brad's voice shattered my thoughts. He was trying to look and sound teasing, I knew, but his smile was forced.

"That's up to you, babe." My tone was teasing, too. "Sondra's cute, right?"

He snorted. "Cute like hell." He coughed and looked uncomfortable. "Not that it matters. You know me. I wouldn't do ... um ... even if ... uh. Well. You know what I mean." That was the way it'd been since I told him about the wife-swap thing. He alternated between seeming to like the idea, to stuttering over his words, to pretending to be shocked and swearing his undying devotion to me. His confusion only proved that I was the true master. He didn't have a clue how to handle this curve ball I'd thrown him.

I rubbed his shoulder. "I know what you mean. Believe me, I know just how trustworthy you are."

His uncomfortable look only intensified. "But, sweetheart, you're not actually gonna do it with ..." he trailed off unable to finish.

"Babe, please. You can trust me." I pulled him closer to me and pressed my body into his. "I won't do anything that you wouldn't do."

The light from the chandelier suddenly ricocheted off the sequins on Beth's dress, drawing my eye to her. Her lovely silver off-the-shoulder gown was a far cry from the sad T-shirt and broken flip-flops she had worn her first day. I had changed her for the good, fashion-wise. And wasn't that something to be proud of? I'd made her into a mom worthy of our 'hood. No doubt I'd changed her in other less obvious ways too. She would never be naïve again. And wasn't that good too? After all, naïveté can be dangerous.

I scanned her face from across the room, but she didn't look worried. Had she developed a knack for the poker face? Or did she truly not know what would happen later?

What Brian was expecting? I'd given him to understand that Beth would be very happy if he would provide the full ... well, Monty. I told him she might deny she wanted it, but if so, it was only an act. A way of saying she wasn't that kind of girl. But I'd insisted that she really was that kind; she just might need a little convincing.

Brian had been highly accommodating. Even eager. Now I looked him over in all his bulky ugliness. How had he managed such a transformation in so few years? It was hard to believe he was the same age as Brad. He'd been quite the hunk back in the day. But now? He was a hunk alright—a hunk of cellulite and broken dreams. He was a pathetic has-been, full of borrowed arrogance from a long-forgotten time. He was perfect for Beth.

I glanced briefly at Brian's wife. I wondered how he got her to agree to this. She looked like a stuffy prude. But then, he probably lied and said he wasn't going through with it. I doubted she'd even think of doing anything with her beau for the night. That's just one of the reasons I gave her to Brad. That and I knew he wouldn't want her. He might be a lying cheat but he had standards.

Just then, my eyes met Beth's. She looked hastily away, and I caught her wiping a tear out of her eye. She did know what awaited her after all. Knowing that, I had no need to force the smile that spread over my face.

THE KING BEE

I think the wife has gone off her rocker. I mean what the hell? She actually wants me to sleep with another woman? I don't get it. Sure, I already slept with lots before her and well, lots after, but I assumed she was in the dark about that. But now, what does this mean? Does she know something? Or just suspect?

And is she planning to sleep with that Hispanic guy, just to get even with me? But would she really do that? Not only have an affair but an affair with a Latino dude? That didn't seem Elise's style. But I knew she was the one who made the matchups. She could tell me about her complicated computer program, but I knew it was her. Her choices and her rules. Always. And frankly, it was getting old.

Then why give me that woman to sleep with? Any of the other women would have been a pleasure. Have already been a pleasure, in some cases. But, okay, I can kind of see her reasoning. I guess she's giving me the ugly one so—for once—I won't actually do anything. But maybe I could surprise her on that score at least.

I gave Sondra a once-over, looking for any possible reason to do this thing. I could find damn little incentive. Still, I'd be stuck with her for the night. Maybe with the lights off and my eyes closed ...

I shuddered. I didn't think I could do it. Unless I got drunk. I looked at her again. Really drunk. I grabbed some champagne from a waiter and downed it in one gulp. Then I headed to the bar. I needed something stronger.

THE INFORMER

The night wore on slowly. This party or ball—whatever Elise wanted to call it—was even more tedious than most. I just wanted to get it over with. I was ready to be done with it and with her. For so long I'd fought it, hanging on with everything I had. But now in a few short hours, maybe even less, it would all be thrown away. All my hard work, all my hopes and dreams for my daughter would be down the drain.

And yet, I couldn't really be sad. I guess I'd known all along deep down what I'd been doing wasn't worth it. Finally I was daring to go down a different path. What would it mean for my daughter? I didn't know for sure, but some things I could guess. She would lose the privileged place I'd been buying for her. Now, she'd either have to earn it herself some way or she'd have to be part of the lesser crowd. Dare I say it? She might even be in with the nerds. But was that really so bad? After all, I'd survived. And she would too. Maybe she'd even be stronger, and smarter, because of it.

I pushed away thoughts of my daughter. I thought of her majesty now. How would she feel later tonight? I would love to be a fly on the wall in her room. I was going to enjoy this. After everything Elise had put me through, I was going to savor my moment on top. Especially since I knew just how fleeting it would be.

THE TARGET

I caught Elise watching me, her brows drawn together. I guessed she wondered why I didn't look worried. So, I arranged my face into a suitably scared expression. Even feigned some tears. Funny to think that now I'd become a good actress, when it was too late.

Or almost. There was one act still to be played. I was

beginning to understand her now. Like I'd known she would, she picked Rick for herself. Obviously, she expected me to be torn up with jealousy. Little did she know she'd only played into my hands.

Now that her posse had deserted her, she was acting on her own. And though it was an admirable show of something—determination, audaciousness, or maybe just desperation—clearly she was a woman who thrived when she had backup. Now, with none, she wasn't the same. She just didn't know it. Yet.

THE QUEEN BEE

Finally it was showtime. The minor guests were gone, the ballroom was by now no doubt being stripped of all evidence of the night: leftover food, flowers, and decorations vanishing as if they never existed. Yet, other aspects of this night would last. I planned to make sure of that.

I went into my room. Rick, my date for the night, was already there, I figured, since the shower was running. How sweet. He was making himself all freshly clean for me. Brad never did that. He acted like his sweat was an aphrodisiac.

Well, if Rick was making an effort, I would too. I opened my suitcase and took out my sexiest nightgown—classy, but low cut and totally see-through—and put it on. I knew no guy could resist me in this number. Although I suspected Rick wasn't the kind of guy to give in without a fight, I knew I'd win in the end. He was, after all, just a man.

I lay down on the bed and arranged myself to ultimate advantage. True, I had no bad side, but I checked the mirror and made sure he'd be able to see not only the real me but my reflection, if he tried to look away.

The shower stopped and my heart beat faster. With surprise, I realized it was from nerves. It had been a while since I'd been with anyone but Brad. Still, back in the day there'd been a decent number of guys. I'd been no slouch. Where was the old confidence? It couldn't desert me now. Especially because he'd be out any minute.

The lock clicked and the doorknob turned. This was it. I stuck my chest out for maximum effect and then there he was. But it was all wrong. It wasn't Rick. It was Brian. Big, ugly, and extremely creepy Brian, who leered at me and then staggered toward me as if he were on a cruise ship during a hurricane. He tripped on my suitcase and suddenly he was on top of me, kissing my neck and pawing me with his hands. I screamed and struggled. I didn't know how it happened, but somehow, some way, I'd ended up in the very place Beth should've been.

RONNIE

I walked into my assigned room for the night. Steve was already there. He started and stopped suddenly, giving the impression he'd been pacing the room.

"Oh, hey, Ronnie." His voice was odd—kind of shaky and wobbly sounding.

"Hey, Steve." I looked at him closer. His eyebrow was twitching and an Adam's apple I never noticed before was bobbing.

"Hey." He coughed. "Um." Coughed again. "So." Almost coughed a third time, but stopped himself mid-cough.

"So."

We were both quiet. Our eyes met almost accidentally. He looked away like they'd touched fire.

"Steve ... is there a problem?"

He sighed. "Shit, yeah. This thing here is so fu ..." He stopped and cleared his throat. "Look, I'm just going to ask you straight out. I mean, what exactly are you expecting here?"

Then I knew what was going on. So I couldn't help saying what I did. "Isn't it obvious? I expect you to serve it up, dude. So, let's get to it."

He turned pale and held up his hands in a defensive position, like I was going to jump him or something. At that sight, I couldn't hold back anymore. The laughter just poured out of me.

He put his hands down, looking both relieved and annoyed. "Very funny."

Suddenly something struck me as decidedly unfunny. "Thanks, Steve. For making it so clear how repulsive you think I am."

He looked uncomfortable. "Ronnie, I don't think you're repulsive. You're an attractive woman." He gave me a look that said, how could I not know that? "I just ... it's not my idea of ... it's not cool. You know?"

I sighed my agreement. "Yeah. I do know. But why did you look so nervous before?"

He looked like he didn't want to answer. But after a few beats of silence he did. "It's just that I didn't know what you expected. I thought if you might want me to ...

you know ... but then if I didn't, I didn't want it to get back to anyone. You know—that I wimped out."

I raised my eyebrows. He was such a guy. Or worse, he was such a male sidekick version of his lovely wife. "You mean if it got back to Brad."

"Not just him. Or like the guys at the station."

"How would they know about this?"

"I don't know. It could get out somehow."

"Well, don't worry. Your secret is safe with me."

Now he raised his eyebrows but remained silent.

"What?"

"Um, Ronnie, you're not exactly known for keeping secrets."

I felt a surge of anger, but I let it pass because he had a point. "Well. I've changed. Gone over to the light. If anyone asks me about tonight, I'll say it was the best sex of my life. And you can do the same. Deal?"

"Let's not overdo it ..."

"Oh, by the way, do you have any distinguishing birthmarks? An embarrassing tattoo perhaps?" I paused, thinking of other possibilities. "Some horrible accident to your privates? If so, you should show me now so I can prove we did it."

He turned pale again. It was too easy to mess with him. Was he actually a cop? "Joking."

He gave a lame chuckle. "Glad you're enjoying this so much."

"Sorry. I guess I'm just relieved we feel the same way about this."

"Yeah. Me too."

I was relieved. And happy. In fact, I almost wanted to confide in him about everything. But that was against the rules. Or wait … those were the old rules. This was a new ball game with a brand-new umpire.

GAIL

Okay. So I admit it. For a wild moment I was tempted to see this thing through. And not for once because of any raging hormones. Actually, they had subsided enough that a man like Ian really wasn't tempting. In fact, I think I could even resist Brad now.

No, I toyed briefly with the thought for the sake of revenge. Ronnie had slammed me so many times by telling my secrets for maximum embarrassment. And didn't that deserve some payback?

But the sane part of me knew sleeping with her husband would be more payback than her actions deserved. And it wouldn't only be hurting her—it would be hurting a person I'd already hurt, and I wouldn't do that to Joe. Not again.

I didn't know what Ian was expecting, but I was sure he wasn't the cheating type.

Sure enough, I no sooner walked through the door, than he started talking. "Gail, um, this isn't my thing. I mean I was going to stay home, but Ronnie …"

I held up my hand. "No worries, Ian. We're totally on the same page."

He looked relieved. "Oh, good. So. Um. You wanna watch TV?"

I laughed. "Sure."

We sat down, on separate beds even, and settled in for a safely boring evening. In fact, I felt like I was at home with Joe. They both surfed through the channels in the same annoying way. Finally he stopped on some sports show, looking at me with raised brows. I shrugged. At least he was asking my opinion. Joe never did.

But I didn't care. My mind wasn't on the TV. It was on the others. I hoped the pieces were coming together. But it was out of my control. I just had to wait and be ready.

I guess I dozed off and then it happened. Pandemonium. Confusion. Screaming. Half naked people. And Elise in middle of it. It was a beautiful sight to behold.

KELLY

So, Joe and I came to an understanding. But not before he took me totally by surprise. By the way he walked in the room, I knew he was drunk. But I still didn't expect it when he grabbed me and planted his lips on mine. I pushed him off me and stepped back, shocked. That was so not like him.

Then his shoulders slumped, and he almost looked like he was going to cry.

There was some awkward silence and he sat down wearily. It was so quiet I could hear his breathing. "Um, Kelly. Sorry about that." He gestured with his hand to where we'd been standing.

"It's okay." It wasn't, but it's what you say in those situations. Not that I'd been in this situation before.

"No. It's not okay."

"You just surprised me. I didn't think you would ..."

"I know. I ... look. Gail and I have been having some problems. And I thought I could do this because ... well, anyway. Turns out I can't." He looked up at me and quickly added, "I mean, I can do it. There's nothing wrong with me or anything."

I rolled my eyes. Guys were so funny.

"But you probably wouldn't want to anyway. Not with me."

I didn't want to hurt his feelings, but he was right. I didn't. I guess my silence told him that.

He nodded as if I'd spoken. But frankly my mind was already moving from him and on to more important matters. Soon, the shit would hit the fan. And I needed to mentally prepare for the explosion.

BETH

It had turned out easier than I thought possible. It was easy to convince Brian in his drunken state that Elise actually wanted him. That she was expecting him even. Elise hadn't planned this as well as her minions would have. Ronnie wouldn't have left so many loopholes or made it so easy to mess up her plans. I'd gotten the key to Elise's room and then slipped it to Brian. Elise just assumed the guys would go to their respective rooms. She never even considered the possibility that someone wouldn't follow her orders.

Soon the final card would be played. Was I ready? To face her wrath? I wasn't sure. But I'd find out soon enough.

Rick must have read some of my emotions on my face. He walked over to me and ran his hands up and down my arms. "I'm proud of you, Beth."

I laughed nervously. "Proud? Yeah, right."

He didn't return the laugh. "Yes, proud. Because you're standing up to her." He paused, looking me in the eye. "I'm sorry. I didn't know what was going on. What she was putting you through."

"You weren't supposed to. None of the guys knew."

"I guess we're kind of stupid, huh?"

"Maybe just naïve. At least when it comes to queen bees."

"So. What happens when this is over?"

"We can start again, somewhere else. Or ... if she's taken down as completely as we hope, we might not have to. Either way, things will be better."

He nodded.

Then we heard it. Screaming and the sound of people running in the halls. Almost like we were under attack. And we might well be.

ELISE

It had taken all my strength to get Brian off me, but even then it might not have been enough except that he was so drunk. And surprised—I got the feeling he hadn't expected me to resist. When I shoved him hard, he tumbled to the floor, laying there in a heap.

I bolted off the bed and went for the door.

But when I glanced back I saw he was still on the floor. He sat up, wobbly like, and scratched his head. "What's the problem?"

He didn't seem like a threat now, so I answered him. "How can you ask that? What are you doing here? You're not my partner for the night."

"I know, I wasn't. Not at first. But the other lady—I forgot her name—she told me that you were okay with this. That you wanted this—er, well, you know, me."

What? Someone had messed with my careful plans? One of my own set this up? I felt cold hard fear creeping its way through me. No, that had to be a mistake. Brian was just drunk and confused. No one would dare. Would they?

Suddenly, I could not be in that room another second. I needed air. I threw the door open.

The first thing I saw was Gail staring at me from her doorway just a few feet away. I hurried over, my legs feeling like Jell-O.

"Gail, what the hell is going on?" My voice sounded horrible—strained and high pitched. I barely recognized it as my own.

"What took you so long, Elise?" Her voice was smooth, calm, and steady. "And, I'm sorry, what do you mean?"

That infuriated me. I was the smooth one, damn it. "What do I mean?" I screamed. "Do you have any idea what's going on?"

She stared at me without fidgeting or picking at her nails or anything. "Actually, yeah. I think I have a pretty good idea."

"Gail," I hissed, "aren't you forgetting something? Do you know who you're dealing with?"

"Yeah. I do." She shrugged. "I just don't give a shit anymore." She turned as if to close the door, but then turned back. "Oh, there's something I've been meaning to say to you for a long time. Fuck you."

I went after her, about to shake some sense into her,

but suddenly someone grabbed me from behind. It was actually Ian, holding me back. I didn't think he had it in him.

I shrugged him off and he let me go. I pulled myself up to my full height, my shoulders back. I had more dignity than this. I wouldn't sink to their level. I'd go find my other friends. My true friends.

I walked away and went to Ronnie's door. I knocked. Waited. Knocked again.

Finally, she came to the door looking bored and annoyed. She pulled her hotel robe around herself tighter as if afraid it might show too much skin. "Yes?" She sounded like I was a Girl Scout selling cookies. And like she'd just been doing something decidedly un-Girl Scout–like and resented the interruption.

"Ronnie, please." That sounded too desperate. I tried again. "I mean, something isn't right here. There's been a problem ..."

"Elise, I'm kind of busy here, if you get my drift. But I have to tell you, this was a great idea. Sorry if things aren't working out for you. But I for one am enjoying myself." Before I could say another word, her door slammed in my face.

I felt rising hysteria again. Calm. Just calm yourself. Go to the one who'd never desert you. I found my way to Kelly's door.

She answered my knock right away. "Hey, Elise." She sounded like we'd just met somewhere casually. Like we were going to have our nails done or something.

"Kel. look, I need your help. Something's gone completely wrong. Somehow Brian ..."

But then I saw it in her eyes. She knew. She knew and

didn't care. I recognized the cold look on her face. The icy stare. It was a look I knew well. In fact, I'd perfected it. I backed away horrified. This had to be a nightmare. I pinched myself. Wake up. Wake up. But no matter how hard I pinched, my reality stayed the same.

I'd go to Brad. He could help me. I went to his door. I knocked and knocked but no one came. Fine. I would do this alone. I'd go and face the other one. The last one. The one who caused all these problems. Before she showed up everything was perfect.

I went to Beth's door and pounded. She answered right away like she'd been waiting and knew I'd show up. A quick scan of her face told me how ready she was for me. She looked like she could handle anything I threw her way. Where the hell had she found such sudden confidence when mine was evaporating before my eyes?

I lost it.

My fist shot out and had she not shifted quickly I would have hit her square on the nose, instead I just swiped her ear. But more punches followed along with kicking, and kneeing, and scratching. Whatever I thought of, I did. Unfortunately, one of my best shots—a kick to the groin— landed squarely on Rick, as I glimpsed him doubling over in pain. Where did he come from? Stepped in to protect his wife, I guessed.

So, where the hell was Brad? Why wasn't he protecting me? Blind fury pulsed through me anew.

Suddenly I was pulled away and my arms were yanked behind me. Over my shoulder, I saw Steve.

"Oh, thank God, Steve. Everyone's against me right now."

"It's okay, I got you." I heard a clicking sound. I tried

to move my hands but couldn't. Finally I realized it was because they were in handcuffs.

"What the hell are you doing?"

"Just my job, ma'am."

"Ma'am?" That was the final straw. "Steve, how could you?" I wailed.

Another officer appeared out of nowhere and they tried to drag me away.

I fought against them. "What are you arresting me for? People like me have rights." This could not be happening. This stuff happened to others—people like ... Rick. Not to people like me.

Steve refused to look at me. The other officer answered my question. "Assault. You kicked that gentleman in the groin."

I scoffed. "He's no gentleman."

Just then Brad walked out of his room. He had a towel wrapped around him and he was smoking. He looked me over with an amused glance. "Hey, babe. Great idea. You know, Sondra was actually good." That's all I remember. Because then everything went black. Blissfully, peacefully, black.

CHAPTER EIGHTEEN

BETH

"So, how does it feel, Dorothy? You did it. You killed her. The wicked witch is dead." Ronnie raised her coffee mug to me in a kind of toast.

"She's alive. I didn't kill her." I picked up my coffee mug and took a long sip.

"Sadly, no. But metaphorically speaking you did. She'll never be the same again. The queen bee is dead. And I want to know how it feels. Because I need to live vicariously through you right now."

I sighed. "I hate to disappoint you but honestly it doesn't feel that good. In fact, I almost feel sorry for her."

She raised her eyebrows. "Really? Then you're a better person than me. But I guess I always knew that."

"I don't know about that. A better person wouldn't have needed revenge."

"That wouldn't have been a better person. That would have been a saint. And they're in short supply these days." She paused then asked an unexpected question. "You think there's hope for me?"

"Sure. You're not a lost cause. You've proved that."

"And ..." She hesitated but then went on. "What about us ... being friends?"

I shook my head. "I think we should start fresh. All of us. And do things right this time."

"Just curious—what did you do wrong?"

"Same thing we all did—allowed her to have too much power over us, when she shouldn't have had any."

She nodded. "True. Well, we can hope our daughters don't make the same mistakes we did."

"We can always pass down what we've learned."

"Which they won't listen to."

I laughed. "Some things you have to learn for yourself I guess."

"You know, life is going to be so much different for me now. How will I survive without scheming and playing pranks?"

I laughed again. "I think Ian's going to have his hands full."

She got serious. "No. I think I'm done. I'll be good, as boring as that sounds."

"Good luck with that." I winced. "I didn't mean that sarcastically ..."

But she just laughed. "No. You're right. I will need luck. It won't be easy. Old habits die hard, I'm sure. But they will die, I'll see to that."

Jessie ran in. "Mommy, Brianna just called me. She wanted me to come over and play. But I said no."

Ronnie raised her eyebrows, sharing a look with me. I was pretty sure Jessie had never said no to Brianna before. "Not that I mind but I'm curious. Why'd you say no?"

Jesse shrugged. "Brianna's really bossy. Always telling me what to do and what we should play. Selena said the same thing."

Ronnie and I shared another look. We didn't have to say anything. But if I put our thoughts into words it would have been something like, "The kids will be alright."

ABOUT ATMOSPHERE PRESS

Atmosphere Press is an independent, full-service publisher for excellent books in all genres and for all audiences. Learn more about what we do at atmospherepress.com.

We encourage you to check out some of Atmosphere's latest releases, which are available at Amazon.com and via order from your local bookstore:

Tree One, a novel by Fred Caron

Connie Undone, a novel by Kristine Brown

A Cage Called Freedom, a novel by Paul P.S. Berg

Giving Up the Ghost, essays by Tina Cabrera

Family Legends, Family Lies, nonfiction by Wendy Hoke

Shining in Infinity, a novel by Charles McIntyre

Buildings Without Murders, a novel by Dan Gutstein

What?! You Don't Want Children?: Understanding Rejection in the Childfree Lifestyle, nonfiction by Marcia Drut-Davis

Katastrophe: The Dramatic Actions of Kat Morgan, a young adult novel by Sylvia M. DeSantis

Peaceful Meridian: Sailing into War, Protesting at Home, nonfiction by David Rogers Jr.

SEED: A Jack and Lake Creek Book, a novel by Chris S. McGee

The Testament, a novel by S. Lee Glick

Southern. Gay. Teacher., nonfiction by Randy Fair

Mondegreen Monk, a novel by Jonathan Kumar

ABOUT THE AUTHOR

Barbara Altamirano traded office politics for neighbor-hood politics when she left her job at a large insurance company to become a stay-at-home mom. Adjusting to her new gig in suburbia prompted her to dabble in writing therapy which led to her discovery of a love of writing. Her essays have been published in several places such as *Guideposts Magazine, WOW! Women On Writing* and *bioStories. The Mommy Clique* is her first novel.

CPSIA information can be obtained
at www.ICGtesting.com
Printed in the USA
FSHW021559020720
71569FS